PENGUIN BOO

ANYWHERE

Jon Robinson was born in Middlesex in 1983. When he's not writing, he works for a charity in central London. Find out more about Jon at:
www.facebook.com/jonrobinsonbooks

Books by Jon Robinson

NOWHERE

ANYWHERE

ANYWHERE

JON ROBINSON

PENGUIN BOOKS

PENGUIN BOOKS

Published by the Penguin Group
Penguin Books Ltd, 80 Strand, London WC2R ORL, England
Penguin Group (USA) Inc., 375 Hudson Street, New York, New York 10014, USA
Penguin Group (Canada), 90 Eglinton Avenue East, Suite 700, Toronto, Ontario, Canada M4P 2Y3
(a division of Pearson Penguin Canada Inc.)
Penguin Ireland, 25 St Stephen's Green, Dublin 2, Ireland
(a division of Penguin Books Ltd)
Penguin Group (Australia), 707 Collins Street, Melbourne, Victoria 3008, Australia
(a division of Pearson Australia Group Pty Ltd)
Penguin Books India Pvt Ltd, 11 Community Centre,
Panchsheel Park, New Delhi – 110 017, India
Penguin Group (NZ), 67 Apollo Drive, Rosedale, Auckland 0632, New Zealand
(a division of Pearson New Zealand Ltd)
Penguin Books (South Africa) (Pty) Ltd, Block D, Rosebank Office Park,
181 Jan Smuts Avenue, Parktown North, Gauteng 2193, South Africa

Penguin Books Ltd, Registered Offices: 80 Strand, London WC2R ORL, England

www.penguin.com

First published 2014
001

Text copyright © Jon Robinson, 2014
All rights reserved

The moral right of the author has been asserted

Set in 10.5/15.5pt Sabon LT Std
Typeset by Jouve (UK), Milton Keynes
Printed in Great Britain by Clays Ltd, St Ives plc

British Library Cataloguing in Publication Data
A CIP catalogue record for this book is available from the British Library

ISBN: 978-0-141-34657-1

www.greenpenguin.co.uk

MIX
Paper from
responsible sources
FSC® C018179

Penguin Books is committed to a sustainable
future for our business, our readers and our planet.
This book is made from Forest Stewardship
Council™ certified paper.

Prologue

The butterfly was on fire. It fluttered wildly through the air, leaking coils of smoke from its smouldering ochre wings.

Who had done this? She thrust out her hand to extinguish the flames, but the creature dipped nimbly through her fingers. *I'm trying to help you!* she urged it desperately, and tried again but it was still too quick to capture.

She followed it with her eyes, not blinking, and before long she realized that the butterfly was travelling the same path over and over, caught in some strange loop.

It was trapped.

She waited, anticipating its next movement, and made a grasp for it. The instant her fingers found the flame, she shuddered awake.

'Pyra –'

Pyra looked around with a sharp intake of breath. The windscreen wipers of the silver sports car whined back and forth, smearing the rain-speckled window.

Anton, a black man in his early thirties with a single

glistening stud in his ear, was touching her arm. 'Talking in your sleep again,' he clarified.

'Was I?'

'Yep. Shouting. Everything all right?'

'I think so,' said Pyra.

She rubbed her eyes and shivered, looking outside. An endless froth of white clouds bruised with grey smothered the Scottish countryside.

'How far are we?' she said, rearranging her short spiky black hair.

'Dunno. An hour? Maybe a bit less. You wanna tell me about this dream?'

Pyra thought for a moment. 'I don't . . . I don't really remember.' She sighed, plucking grumpily at the seatbelt strap, which had left a deep pink groove in her neck, and wriggled in her seat.

Anton dug his hand around in the side compartment and removed a cassette tape in a battered cardboard sleeve. 'Let's have a bit of music,' he said, shoving it into the player.

'As long as it's not that annoying piano crap. God, I hate jazz.'

'Yeah,' he said disappointedly. 'Well, I'm working on that.'

'Keep working. I don't get it.'

'No one gets jazz,' he said with a grin, adjusting the volume. 'It gets *you*.'

Pyra smiled with the corner of her mouth. 'You want me to take over for a bit?'

'Not yet.' He tapped the indicator and let the vehicle drift into the next lane. He looked across at her. 'If you're worried about the escaped boy,' he said, 'don't be. We'll find him, Pyra.'

The traffic up ahead quickly became congested. Pyra wound the window down and stretched. The air was damp and cool against her face. 'It looks like some kind of roadblock. You think someone's trying to delay us?'

'Maybe. I guess they figured we'd be on our way.'

As their car inched forward, Anton lowered his window and called to a workman in a fluorescent yellow vest. 'What's going on?' he said. 'When'll we be moving?'

The man shrugged, exhaling a stream of misty air from his red cheeks. 'It's the police. Random vehicle check. Had a tip-off about some illegal goods being smuggled or something.'

A knife of panic stabbed Pyra, and she felt the car becoming airless. 'The stuff in the boot,' she whispered. 'You know, the –'

'It's fine. They won't find it. And even if they do, so what?'

It won't take much to raise their suspicion, Pyra thought.

'You need to relax,' Anton said, but Pyra thought she could see some concern in his eyes too as the car in front rolled a little further forward.

The police officers were talking among themselves. One of them, a bald man with authoritatively piercing blue eyes, waved the next car on. A second officer with a radio went round to the boot of the car and opened it. After some moments he nodded to his colleague, who gestured with his head for the car to move.

The police officer waved Anton and Pyra forward. Pyra watched as a uniformed woman walked over to the window. 'What's all this about?' Pyra asked.

'Just a check, madam,' the policewoman said with rehearsed composure. 'My colleague will check the boot, then you can both be on your way, all right? We don't want to waste any more of your time.' She stepped to the side and whispered into her radio.

'He's going to see,' Pyra hissed to Anton, watching the police officer with narrowed eyes. She slipped an ivory domino out of her pocket and began rolling it across her knuckles.

'You don't need the Ability,' he whispered. 'Remember what Luthan said about getting too reliant?'

'Yeah, well, this is different,' she spat. 'This is an emergency.'

Anton quietened her with a pass of his hand.

The police officer opened the boot and peered inside. There was nothing in there except an old, tattered blanket.

Anton moved his fingers round the steering wheel. He turned his eyes to the wing mirror. Only the elbow of the officer's fluorescent jacket was visible.

The officer was about to close the boot when something urged him to reach towards the blanket.

Anton peered back out of the window. 'Look, how long is this gonna take? We really have to be somewhere . . .'

The policewoman returned to his door. She put a hand on the ridge of the lowered window and leant down. 'Please try to be patient, sir.'

Anton looked in the rear-view mirror. 'I don't understand what you're looking for.'

'That's not any of your business, I'm afraid, sir.' She glared at him and then stepped away from the car.

Pyra was still fiddling with the domino, weaving it over and round her fingers. It wasn't working. She'd left it too late, and now she couldn't concentrate.

'There's nothing back there. You're wasting your time,' said Anton.

The officer lifted the blanket in the boot. Beneath it were several small canvas bags, large enough to slip snugly over a human head, some coils of rope and two tasers.

The policewoman put her radio back in her belt and walked over to the car. 'I'm sorry, sir, but I'm afraid I'm going to have to ask you to –'

Anton slammed his foot on to the accelerator with as much force as he could muster. The nearby police officers leapt out of the way of the speeding car. Then the vehicle burst through a barrier and swerved through a procession of cones, which spilled like skittles.

Pyra looked over her shoulder. 'They're coming after us.'

Anton yanked the gearstick back. The car splashed through a stretch of puddles. Three sirens began to wail as one. Anton slammed the steering wheel to the side. The car spun left from the dual carriageway on to a narrow, winding road, steeped with bracken on either side.

Pyra closed her eyes, plunging into a deep state of concentration, using the domino to help her focus.

Moments later, the police car behind theirs careered on a patch of ice. The driver struggled to reclaim the steering wheel as the car veered into the undergrowth, blocking the route for the following vehicles.

'Guess I was wrong,' Anton said. 'We did need it after all.'

The twenty-three-year-old girl sitting beside him stared silently at the road ahead. The look in her eyes was probably relief, but may also have been excitement.

1

'I understand this is going to come as a bit of a shock, but despite our best efforts there's been an ... unexpected problem with the programme,' said James Felix, the wealthiest man in the country and the leader of the Pledge, into the answering machine. 'Six of the inmates have escaped and are loose in the forest. There's no need to worry about anything just yet, Prime Minister. This is one of the reasons we insisted on such an isolated location and let's not forget that we have some of our best men out looking for them ... and the inmates haven't the faintest where they're going.'

There was a momentary pause while he organized his thoughts.

'We expect this matter will be wrapped up quickly, with little fuss, but I and the rest of the Pledge are keen to hear from you, to know that we still have your support. I'll be in touch as soon as I have further news on the matter. There is no way out of this, Prime Minister. You and the Pledge are in it together. There is no way out,' he repeated.

With that, the voicemail message ended and the phone, in the secret compartment under the floorboards of the prime minister's office, gave a final bleep.

'The stream ends here!' Elsa puffed and pointed to where the sheen of cloudy ice merged with a snow-covered thicket as the pair hurried alongside the steep edge. The canopy of trees quivered gently overhead, shielding them from all but a few falling snowflakes.

Elsa and Harlan had become separated from Ryan and Jes and had been following the ice downhill for an age.

'We should wait for the others,' Elsa said, and brushed her frizzy brown hair out of her eyes. Her usually pale features, covered with freckles, were tinged red with cold. *We're in the middle of a forest, miles from anywhere and we don't have a clue where we're going,* she thought.

Harlan, a tall, slim Indian boy, leant against a tree. 'The guards won't be far behind.' He looked at the distant column of black smoke rising from the crashed truck that they'd used to escape from their prison, then he bent down to tie his shoelace. Finding it too hard to tie a knot with his unresponsive, frozen hands, Harlan shoved the length of lace into the side of his boot and straightened. His black hair was pressed flat against his forehead. 'We need to keep going. We'll find something soon enough.'

'And you know this how?'

'I just *do*. It's hard to explain. I'll tell you some other time.'

'Why don't you tell me now? It's not like I'm going anywhere.'

Harlan lowered his eyes.

'Go on, Harlan,' Elsa insisted. 'I'm all ears. You're always saying stuff like this – that you have these *feelings* –'

'Look, Elsa, I know you're grumpy and you're scared, but taking it out on me isn't going to make things any better –'

'I'm taking it out on you cos you're full of it, Harlan. You don't know anything!'

Harlan glared at her and pressed on. Elsa began muttering to herself when a sudden crack shattered the silence and echoed in the wind for some moments. 'Harlan – what was that?'

'For someone who doesn't know anything, you expect a lot from me, Elsa.'

He cautiously removed the ibis from inside his coat. The weapon was a black metal cylinder, about thirty centimetres in length. Simple and elegant in its design, the ibis was an extremely advanced weapon, able to fire pulses of paralysing compressed sound.

Harlan saw that the power light above the handgrip had dimmed. 'It's not working,' he said, jabbing at the trigger. 'Try yours.'

'Mine's not working either. It's like they've been turned off –'

There was a second shot. Elsa dropped her ibis into the snow. '*Run!*' she cried.

Harlan looked back towards the sound a final time and then ran, with Elsa in close pursuit. The pair sped on until a flailing Harlan tripped, staggered and stumbled.

'Get up,' Elsa pleaded, pulling at his coat. 'Get up, get up, before they catch us.'

'I think we're OK,' he wheezed, wiping his face with his sleeve.

Elsa doubled over by a tree, struggling to reclaim her breath from her pounding heart, which seemed to be beating it out of her. She exhaled, and clutched her stomach. 'It sounded like a gun,' she said. 'Is that what it sounded like to you?'

Harlan kept quiet, although he suspected she might be right. When Elsa eventually stood upright, she spotted something among the trees. 'Look.'

He followed the trajectory of her finger to a small grey hut. 'Cables,' Harlan said, and started towards it.

'Harlan . . .'

Harlan ignored Elsa and tiptoed across to the door. He gave it a gentle push and the door slowly withdrew.

'There's an electricity generator in there. Maybe it's some sort of back-up generator for the prison,' he said, and brushed inside, immediately noticing an indistinct mud pattern on the floor. 'Footprints.' He looked down at his own boot and compared the patterns. 'One of ours.'

'Alyn must've stayed here when he escaped!' Elsa realized.

Harlan mulled it over. 'We should probably rest here for a couple of hours and see out the worst of the night.'

He hopped on to the desk and sat down to pull off his boot. A pile of snow trickled to the floor.

'What's this?' he said, leaning down and poking at a pile of paper files on the floor before picking one up.

'Dunno,' Elsa said, squinting at the folder. 'Do you think this place is part of Nowhere? Seems pretty far from the prison.'

'Maybe they want to keep it secret from the rest of the guards,' Harlan replied, flicking through a couple of pages before finally tossing it on to the floor. 'It just looks like loads of numbers.'

Elsa glanced over her shoulder at their prints in the snow. It wouldn't be long before they were covered. 'What if they look inside?'

'We just have to hope they call it a night before then,' Harlan replied, shutting the door. 'Whatever happens, I know I'm not being taken back without a fight.'

2

'Let us go,' Ryan begged, looking at Jes, lying on her side in the snow. 'Please . . . if she doesn't get help, she'll die.'

Rayner, a tall, muscular guard with several days' stubble, narrowed his eyes and slipped his finger round the trigger.

Words rushed together on Ryan's lips, but none formed. Jes muttered softly, her face obscured by her long red hair.

'Claude,' said the young guard beside Rayner. 'Come on, put the rifle down.'

'She's not what you think – she's not a bad person,' Ryan went on. Lumps of snow were trapped in his curly blond hair. 'I swear it . . . none of us are. *None of us.*'

'You might have convinced me, had you little animals not killed him,' said Rayner.

'Killed him? Killed who? Hang on, we haven't –'

Rayner pointed the rifle at Ryan's chest. 'You should know by now the innocent act doesn't work with me, Farrell.'

Ryan closed his eyes and braced himself for the impact.

The rifle fired, but was knocked to the side, leaving a steaming hole in the snow just centimetres from Ryan's legs.

Ryan looked up with wide eyes as a bearded man slammed a branch down across Rayner's head. Rayner looked baffled momentarily, and then collapsed wordlessly into a heap.

The guard beside him lifted his ibis, but not before the bearded man had raised and swung the branch back at him and knocked him to the ground. He released it and hurried over to Jes, whose consciousness seemed to be slipping away by the second.

He bent down and picked her up, then made eyes at Ryan, who was still kneeling, too shocked to say anything. 'Are you just going to sit there?'

Ryan didn't need telling twice and sprang up. The bearded man gathered his bearings and began to trot with the girl in his arms.

'Who the hell are you?' Ryan said.

'My name's Henry.'

Jes groaned and tried locating the wound in her side with her fingertips. Her green eyes were failing to focus.

'Hey, it'll be all right,' Ryan called across to her. 'You're going to be OK, Jes.'

Henry turned through the trees and they arrived at a small clearing.

'Where do we go?' asked Ryan, looking around for some indication of where they might be. 'There's nothing in every direction, except –'

'Except down. Here. Hold her for a moment.' He passed Jes to Ryan. Weary and aching, Ryan struggled to hold her in his arms and lowered to his knees, trying his best to keep her head raised. He winced as pain jolted through his ankle, which was still sore from the escape.

'What's going on?' Jes said. 'Are we . . . are we free?'

Ryan gently brushed away the snow from the side of her face. 'We're out of that place, if that's what you mean.'

Henry tore frenziedly at the snow, soon revealing a circular metal cover. He dug his fingers round the sides and, with some effort, levered it away. He took Jes from Ryan's arms and gently placed her over his shoulder. Jes whimpered and gritted her teeth.

'Pull the lid over behind you,' Henry said to Ryan, making his way down precariously.

Ryan swivelled on to the first rung, lowered himself down, then reached up and hoisted the cover back above them.

If I never have to climb another ladder again, it'll be too soon, he thought, remembering the tunnel that had led them into the yard. It was a wonder they'd ever escaped from the prison; something had been on their side, but luck seemed too strong a word.

Henry soon reached the bottom, and a solitary light flickered on.

Ryan followed him down a narrow passageway, every step echoing noisily.

'What is this place?' Ryan asked, and felt himself turning a little queasy at the thought that Henry could be leading them right back to where they'd started.

'This is my home,' Henry said.

The three arrived at a door on the left. Henry nudged it with his boot, and slipped into a small room sideways with Jes in his arms.

Inside, a single bulb hung from the ceiling. There was a table in the centre, and one against the far wall. A sleeping bag was crumpled in the corner, beside a small pile of books, wilted with damp. Henry carried Jes over to the table and gently lowered her on to her back, then went over to a cabinet on the wall.

'I'm Ryan. This is Jes.'

Henry nodded.

'You even know what you're doing, mate?' Ryan asked.

'Not really, no. But if you have any better ideas I'd love to hear them.'

Ryan shook his head and brushed some matted, damp strands of hair from Jes's forehead. 'So why did you save us?'

'Because you were in trouble.' Henry opened a first-aid box and removed a pair of scissors. 'And I'd say you still are.'

'But why were you –'

'I need to concentrate,' Henry said, interrupting him.

And I need answers, Ryan thought, but held his tongue as Henry pinched the blood-soaked material of

Jes's grey uniform with his forefinger and thumb and began cutting.

Henry unscrewed a bottle from the box and dribbled clear fluid on to the wound. Jes writhed and cried out. When Ryan glanced across at Henry, he noticed his hands were trembling as he reached for a pair of forceps.

'She'll try to resist, Ryan. But I need to get that bullet out.'

Henry took a deep breath and lowered the forceps to the wound in Jes's side. Ryan watched with half-closed eyes.

Jes screamed and kicked her legs frantically.

'Ryan, keep her still –'

'Jes, you've got to keep still, you've got to keep still,' Ryan said, watching with horror as the forceps turned red. 'It's OK,' Ryan said, wincing. 'Everything's OK.'

She squeezed Ryan's hand with such force he felt his fingers going cold. And then she was still.

'She's passed out,' Henry said, noticing Ryan's concern. 'It's for the best.'

He delved further with the forceps and then he paused. 'I think I've found it.' He removed them gently. Pinched in their grip was a dripping bullet.

3

As he sprinted through the forest, tears filled Alyn's eyes, dissolving the landscape around him until he could no longer see where he was running.

'*Murderer!*' he'd heard Ryan cry through the radio, and he had listened in disbelief.

He stopped, bent double and leant against a tree, his black fringe hanging into his eyes.

Ryan. It was his fault. He'd got Jes involved, and fed her these stupid ideas that he could free them.

Breathing hoarsely, Alyn knelt down and fumbled in the snow for the heaviest branch he could find. The branch murmured as he lashed it through the air, imagining swinging it at Ryan's face.

'Hey!'

It took Alyn a moment to realize that a voice had called out to him, among the whistling wind and rustling leaves.

He turned to find himself faced with a girl in her early twenties, with black spiky hair. She wore a leather jacket and torn jeans and her eyes were dark with mascara.

'Who – who are you?' he said, lowering the branch.

The girl took a step towards him. 'My name's Pyra. We've been looking for you. I'm part of a very special group. We're –'

'You're with *them*?'

'Look, I don't know who you're talking about,' she went on. 'But we need to take you with us.'

'I'm not going with you,' Alyn said. 'My friends need me.'

'So do we,' Pyra said, removing a taser and pointing it at him with both hands. 'I can't let you leave.'

Alyn looked at the weapon and raised an eyebrow. 'You're threatening me?'

'Yep. Now drop the branch and get over here.'

Alyn loosened his grip on the branch. 'Here,' he said, feigning dropping it while launching it at her hand. Pyra dropped the taser with a yelp as the branch struck her wrist.

Alyn charged at her and tackled her into the snow. He crawled towards the taser, grabbed it and pointed it at her.

'All right, kid.' She sighed, raising her palms in defeat. 'You win. Just chill.'

'You want to take me back there?' Alyn panted, staring at her.

'No.'

In his time at the prison Alyn had come across many liars and wasn't about to be fooled so easily. He moved his finger round the taser, searching for a trigger.

'Prove it,' he said. 'Prove you are who you say you are.'

'I can't prove anything,' Pyra said, lowering her hands. 'Besides, you've already made your mind up.'

Alyn thrust the taser in her direction. 'I swear I'll –'

Pyra met his eyes with some reluctance. 'You don't have any idea why you're here, do you?'

Alyn lowered his eyes. 'No. But I've got a feeling *you* do. And that's what I'm about to find out,' he said.

Pyra smiled coolly.

'I said, *that's what I'm about to –*'

Alyn's words were cut short by something landing across the back of his head, and everything went black.

4

Jes's eyes flickered open and swept around the dark little room. 'Where are we?' she croaked, and her eyes filled with alarm at the stone walls. 'Are we back in Nowhere?'

Ryan sprang to his feet and ran across to the table, grinning at her. 'We're not,' he said. 'We're never going back there.'

Jes turned her head, trying to make sense of her surroundings.

'We're in an underground bunker. It's miles from Nowhere,' Ryan said, sparing her further confusion. 'You all right?'

'You tell me,' she said, bringing a hand to her brow. 'How do I look?'

'You want the truth or –'

'When a girl asks that, she never wants the truth.' She smiled, and wearily closed her eyes. 'I remember a man with a white beard saving us, I think . . .'

'Henry.'

'So I wasn't dreaming. Who is he?'

Some crazy old man living in the forest by the look of

things, Ryan almost said, but was interrupted by the door opening. 'He can tell you himself,' he said, and stood up straight as Henry appeared.

Jes felt her side. She grimaced as her fingers fell on the dressing. 'Thanks for saving us,' she said.

'My pleasure. Though I've never been good at sewing. You're going to have quite a scar.'

'A small price to pay, I guess.'

Henry nodded and carried over a can of water and helped her tilt her head to drink. When she had taken a mouthful, he handed her a small tablet.

'For the pain,' he said. 'So you were both prisoners in there. How did that happen?'

'We were kidnapped,' Ryan said, wiping his nose on his sleeve.

'They told us we were criminals,' Jes added. 'And that it was a detention centre.'

'I need to know *exactly* what happened to you both in that place,' said Henry.

'Chores, jobs,' said Jes, pushing the can back towards him. 'And these weird lessons . . .'

Henry looked intrigued by this. 'Go on,' he urged.

'It was this woman. *Susannah*. She said she was a teacher, but we knew she wasn't. She made us watch these weird education films. They looked like they were from the seventies.'

'They were supposed to make us better people,' Ryan agreed.

'And?'

Jes shrugged. 'And that was it,' she said, then paused. 'Wait a minute, there was something else too – a few of us noticed split-second flashes of random things in the films.'

'What kind of things?' Henry asked.

'Just pictures,' Jes said, wincing with a spasm of pain. 'I don't know. I can't really remember.'

'Try,' Henry said. 'It might give us some idea of what the Pledge has been doing.'

'The Pledge?' Ryan looked at Jes, then back at Henry. 'You mean you've heard of it too?'

'The name has been whispered around for a long time. We weren't even sure it existed. We thought it was just another conspiracy theory. But the Pledge is real. It just keeps itself well hidden.'

'"*We*" being . . .'

'My people,' Henry said, walking back to the door. 'You'll get to meet them soon enough. Until then, you need some rest.' He looked at Ryan. 'And, you, stay put. The forest is still too dangerous.'

Ryan and Jes stayed silent until Henry's footsteps faded.

'So,' Ryan said, turning to Jes but keeping a watchful eye on the door, 'what do you think of Santa back there?'

'Well, he saved us, so I don't want to speak too badly . . .'

'But?'

'But he sounds like one of those people who have spent too long by themselves,' Jes murmured, and looked up at Ryan. 'We should be careful.'

5

Julian had been walking through the night when he stumbled upon the hut.

He removed a lighter he had stolen from the guards and pressed the flint. The flame illuminated the ground, enough for him to see a pair of boot prints carved into the snow.

Clutching the ibis with his other hand, Julian moved quietly to the door. He gave it a gentle tap, but it wouldn't budge; something was blocking it.

There was a soft crack from the undergrowth: a twig, perhaps a branch. Julian released his finger from the flame and the light melted quickly into darkness.

Maybe I should've stayed with the others, he thought as he walked on, but quickly admonished himself. Elsa was too young, too slow – a liability. Ryan was too brash and loud and careless. Harlan lacked common sense and favoured intuition over reason. The only one who might prove worthy of his company was Jes. But she and Alyn were an item and the thought of forging a relationship, no matter how platonic, seemed like a tremendous waste of time and effort when her energies were inevitably directed elsewhere.

Within an hour, the trees parted and Julian found himself shivering at the foot of a field. Wincing as snow rose over his boots and seeped into his already damp trousers, he stomped towards the harder ground. Up ahead, something caught his eye. A signpost.

He trotted towards it and felt around in his pocket for the lighter. The signpost read:

RAILWAY STATION 3 MILES

6

All but one of the Pledge were gathered round a table on the top floor of Pillar, the tallest skyscraper in London's financial district. James Felix, the group's leader, shared a look with the other present members, Antonia and Blythe, then turned his eyes to the clock.

'Stephen will be here soon,' said Antonia, noticing his restlessness.

Antonia was forty-seven, and the heir to one of the largest banking families in Europe. She wore her hair in a short black bob, while years of cosmetic surgery gave her a blank, almost geisha-like expression.

'I don't think he's coming,' Felix muttered, resting a hand on the mahogany table. 'And time isn't on our side.'

'Felix is right,' said Blythe, a fifty-year-old aristocrat. His grey moustache wiggled as he spoke. 'We should at least get something in place before that little devil interferes! Speaking of interfering, where is this adviser of yours, Felix? I expected to see him poking his nose in.'

'Emmanuel's around,' said Felix. 'But the Prime Minister isn't. I've left three messages with him now.'

'A little birdie tells me he's taken a holiday,' said Blythe, cramming a sandwich in his mouth. 'To *Italy*. Not that he has any power anyway.'

'But he *knows*,' said Antonia.

Felix considered this silently and left the table, gliding over to the glass wall. As he did so, the door opened and twenty-one-year-old Stephen Nover, the second-wealthiest man in the country, appeared. Slender and composed, Stephen gently checked his blond parting with a careful pale hand before walking in.

'There he is!' Blythe announced with a stuffed mouth, slapping the table. 'What time do you call this, boy?'

Stephen walked past Blythe and Antonia and dropped into a chair, putting his feet defiantly on the tabletop. A life of privilege had left him with little to show except a smug, entitled pout.

'There's a reason I called this emergency meeting,' Felix said, moving back to the group. 'As you all know, one of our subjects escaped. He wasn't alone. Since then, five more have joined him. It's likely they're all part of the same group. Stephen, are you even listening to me?'

Stephen was staring out of the window, as though rapt. 'A hunt . . .' he murmured softly, not looking away. 'We hunt them.'

'That is the sensible thing to do,' Blythe added,

fiddling thoughtfully with his moustache. 'Still in the woods, are they? Good luck to them making it out of there alive!'

'But we don't want deaths on our hands,' said a sombre Antonia.

Stephen began giggling. The rest of the Pledge looked at him.

'Is something funny?' Felix asked.

Stephen shook his head. He lowered into his chair, making his silk tie dance with a playful forefinger.

Blythe stroked his moustache. 'We'll employ some ... gentlemen to deal with the situation at once. Mercenaries, like the ones we used for the kidnapping. The sort of men who'll do anything if the price is high enough.'

'*All* men will do anything if the price is high enough,' Stephen sneered. 'I don't see what the problem is. I say it'll be good fun.'

'Fun?' Felix looked at the others for verification that he was not hearing things. 'Six escaped subjects on the loose and you think it might be *fun*?'

'Yes. *Fun*. What's wrong? I take it you've never been hunting.'

Antonia crossed her arms. 'That's what you see this as? A hunt? A game? Whoever decided to get you involved in this –'

'Enough.' Felix slammed his hand down on the table. A couple of the glasses rattled. 'Listen to you, bickering like schoolchildren!'

27

'As far as I can see, the schoolboy *is* the problem,' said Antonia.

In the reflection of the window Felix noticed Emmanuel had entered the room. Wearing his usual dark grey suit, with his black hair parted conservatively to the side, he stood eerily still.

'He's right,' Emmanuel said, and every pair of eyes turned to him. 'With them free, there is a chance that everything we have worked for will be lost. We need to find them. And, out of all of you, *he* –' Emmanuel indicated Stephen – 'is most suitable to manage this.'

For all the wrong reasons, Felix very nearly said, glancing across the table. Rumours of Stephen's cruelty from former employees were curiously persistent, and from what he had seen of the boy, Felix was prepared to accept it not merely as hearsay.

'I'm glad one of you has some sense,' Stephen said with a smirk. 'I'll gather up a little hunting party. The escaped subjects have no money, no shelter, no transport. With the guards on their tails and our own men closing in on them, they'll be surrounded!'

'I want it made clear that they are to be returned to the prison *unharmed*,' Felix said.

'I have a better idea,' Stephen went on excitedly. 'Perhaps we should take one as a sacrifice.'

'A sacrifice? What the devil are you talking about?'

'A *warning*,' Stephen clarified, his eyes wide. 'That's what I mean. It'll be a message for the others to stay put. I think it should be that Alyn Hart fellow. They see him as some kind of hero, and there's no better symbol to slay.'

'Now, now, you little rogue, I too draw the line at murder,' Blythe said, brushing crumbs from his trousers. 'But, regardless, let us cross that line if and when we come to it.'

Felix looked around the room. 'Unless anyone has anything else to add, I declare this meeting over.' He tapped the table with his knuckle. '*Semper ad meliora.*'

'*Semper ad meliora,*' the others repeated in unison, except Emmanuel, who was watching Felix intently.

7

After a barely conscious Alyn had had his wrists bound and was dragged into the back of the silver sports car, Pyra wilted into the passenger seat.

'The police will still be looking for us, Anton,' Alyn heard her mutter. 'Guess we should find somewhere to stay for the night. There's a bed and breakfast a few miles south.'

'Sounds good,' replied the driver, Anton, pulling his phone out of his pocket. 'I'm gonna call the others.'

'Don't say too much just yet.' She made eyes at their captive on the back seat. 'He's not ready to know.'

'Not surprised, with what he's been through. I just hope he don't try anything.'

'I'm not gonna try anything,' Alyn answered. *Not yet.* He tugged at the cord round his wrist with his thumb.

Anton held the phone against his ear.

'No answer,' he said with a sigh, and dropped his phone into the cup holder behind the handbrake. Alyn watched helplessly as he yanked his seatbelt across his chest and turned on the ignition.

Who were these people and what did they want with him? The fact they were carrying tasers didn't exactly fill him with optimism. Alyn squinted at the small tattoo on the back of Pyra's neck, barely able to keep his eyes open.

Maybe if I sleep I'll be able to think straight, he considered. *Just for a few minutes. That's all I'll need and then I'll work out what to do next.*

Alyn gazed at the grey sky pouring past the car window and before he knew it he was asleep. His dreams were dark and heavy, pulling him in all directions.

Harlan and Elsa had set off again in the early light.

After an hour of walking, Elsa spotted a thin needle of grey in the snow reflecting the morning winter sun.

'A train track!' she exclaimed, tugging Harlan's sleeve. 'You know what that means?'

Harlan shielded his eyes but Elsa was already speeding towards it. He ran after her, laughing, and stumbling clumsily across the snow on weary legs.

'Come on, Harlan!' She looked over her shoulder and gave an impatient wave, beckoning him to follow.

Elsa sprang over a sagging wire fence. Harlan hopped over, landing in her prints. He reached down and scooped up the ibis, which had fallen from his pocket.

'Look,' he said, showing her the blue light by the trigger. 'I think it's working again.'

'Too bad I threw mine away. It would've been a pretty cool souvenir.'

'A *pretty cool souvenir?* You already forgotten what it felt like to be on the receiving end of one of these?'

'No one would be mean to me in school again,' she said, and imitated firing at an imaginary foe. A part of her almost missed the ibis battles with the guards back in the prison.

Harlan looked concerned. 'Who's mean to you in school?'

Elsa's cheeks darkened. 'No one,' she said. 'I'm just saying, that's all.'

The pair followed the tracks, side by side, for the rest of the morning. The countryside seemed to be repeating itself. Every post or pillar they passed made Elsa think they might be just a little closer to somewhere, but they continued trudging on, not crossing paths with another soul, freezing cold and weak with hunger.

'I'm getting such a headache,' Harlan said, holding a hand across his brow.

The pair rested beneath a tree. Even though seated, Elsa still felt the rhythm of the walk pulsing behind her eyes.

She watched as Harlan dug around inside his pocket and removed a silver coin, tilting it so that the light caught the edge.

'You ever gonna tell me what that means, Harlan?'

'It's a coin,' he said. 'It doesn't mean anything. Come on, let's keep moving.'

The pair had not walked more than a hundred metres

when up ahead, in a clearing beside the track, there was the sloping, tiled roof of a train station.

'Look, people!' said Elsa, spotting a man and woman dressed in thermal hiking clothes. 'We should tell them everything . . . we should tell them what happened to us.'

'Would *you* believe us? We're not telling anyone, just like we all discussed. We need to get out of here without making a fuss.'

They hurried across the snow, brushing past the undergrowth, and hopped on to the elevated stone platform.

'We're really going home, aren't we?' she whispered, her words sounding dazed and disjointed.

'We're not going *home*,' Harlan said. 'We still need to wait for Jes and Ryan in London, like we agreed. Remember?'

'Yeah, if they even turn up – that gunshot didn't sound good.'

Thankful for their coats hiding their grey prison uniforms, the pair smiled politely at the hikers and peered at the train timetable behind a glass display.

'Looks like we'll have to make a few changes,' Harlan said quietly, wiping away the frost. 'I've never heard of half these places.'

'What about money?' Elsa whispered. 'We don't have anything!'

'We'll think of something,' Harlan said uncertainly. 'Now let's just get on a train.'

*

A quarter of an hour later they were away, and the bare bone-white countryside was gliding gently past.

'I've been thinking about that sound,' Elsa said, making distracted squiggles on the foggy window with her fingernail. 'The *gun*. You really think we might be the only ones left?'

Harlan shook his head slowly and shrugged, and Elsa seemed to shrink into her seat at his uncertainty. 'I'm not trying to scare you.'

'Well, you have. You're supposed to say, "Oh no, everyone's fine. It wasn't a gunshot; it was Rayner falling down the hill and breaking his stupid leg."'

Harlan grinned. 'Let's hope you're right about that. I just want you to realize how important this is. We can't make any mistakes –'

'Look who it is,' came a voice from behind them. 'I thought I might see you two here.'

Both Elsa and Harlan jumped as Julian emerged from the aisle.

'Julian?' said Elsa, excited to see a familiar face. 'I could hug you.'

Julian held up a hand in protest. 'I'd rather you didn't.' He sat down beside Harlan. 'I assume you both heard it –'

'Yeah,' said Harlan. 'We heard it.'

'That must mean it's Ryan.' Elsa looked alarmed. 'Or Jes …'

'Or Alyn. Maybe Adler finally caught up with him,' Harlan said.

'Last I saw of Adler, he won't be catching up with anyone,' Julian mumbled, remembering how Jes had snapped and fired her ibis at the defenceless guard repeatedly until he began shaking and eventually fell still.

'What's that supposed to mean?' Elsa looked at Harlan, puzzled, then spotted an elderly ticket inspector rattling slowly down the aisle towards them.

'An inspector,' she said under her breath. 'He'll throw us off if he catches us without tickets. What shall we do?'

Julian smirked. 'Follow me,' he said, and scurried out of his seat.

Harlan looked back over his shoulder as the inspector shuffled closer. The inspector tapped the female hiker on the shoulder, who woke with some alarm and began silently foraging through her bag for her ticket.

Julian pulled open the toilet door and darted inside. Harlan fell in behind him and only just managed to get in before he slammed the door shut.

'Elsa's still outside,' Harlan said. 'If she gets thrown off, I'm going with her.'

He reached for the door but Julian grabbed his hand. 'There's not enough room in here for her as well, no matter how small she is.'

'I'm not leaving her by herself,' Harlan hissed.

Julian elbowed him in the ribs. 'And I'm not leaving this train, so shush!'

They waited for a moment. Then there was a faint cough from the other side of the door. 'Come out, please.'

Julian and Harlan looked at one another.

'After you,' Julian said, gesturing for Harlan to step out.

Harlan hesitantly emerged to meet the inspector's waiting gaze. 'I'm sorry,' he flustered. 'I was just – I –'

'Ticket, please,' the inspector commanded, holding out his hand.

'That's the thing,' Harlan said. 'I just lost my ticket, I –'

Desperate, Harlan looked around and spotted something on the floor by his feet, a scrap of paper. With no other option, Harlan leant down and handed it to the inspector, willing him not to notice that it was nothing but an old receipt. At that moment he felt a little woozy. He put his hand to his head as the train jolted, and the inspector was thrown against the wall.

Staggering, the inspector cursed under his breath and peered out of the window.

'Must've been something on the track,' he mumbled. 'These old trains feel every bump.'

He pushed the useless scrap of paper back towards Harlan and marched back down the carriage, rubbing his shoulder. Harlan released the breath he hadn't realized he'd been holding.

'What were the chances of that?'

'How fortunate,' Julian purred, still inside the toilet. 'Well, I don't see Elsa anywhere. I guess the little runt got caught after all.'

Harlan looked up as a freckled, anxious face peeked out from the overhead luggage compartment.

'Who are you calling "runt"?' she said.

8

It took Alyn a few hazy moments to realize he was lying face down on a dirty carpet in a cheap hotel bedroom with his wrists bound.

His head felt thick and slow, as though moving underwater. *What happened?* he thought, trying to piece together the last hour or so. *Have I been asleep? Did I pass out?*

'You think we should ask the kid what he knows about the Pledge?' he heard Pyra say from across the room.

'Not yet,' Anton answered. 'A little knowledge is a dangerous thing. Don't want to scare him off, do we?'

Alyn kept still, his eyes fixed on the torn wallpaper round the radiator beside him. The wall was streaked with mould.

'Anyway, I'm gonna turn in,' Pyra said. 'See you later.' Her footsteps padded softly across the carpet.

'You could've given me a pillow,' Alyn said weakly some moments after the door closed behind her.

Anton got up. 'Sorry, mate, here you go,' he said, placing a pillow under Alyn's head.

'You could untie me too. I'm not going to run.'

Anton chuckled. 'You must think I'm a fool, Alyn.'

'I can barely feel my hands,' Alyn said. 'Just five minutes.'

The intake of breath suggested Anton might be considering his request. Eventually he gave an indistinct nod and walked over to his prisoner. 'I do have a weapon. Just so you know.'

Alyn squinted at the silver taser. 'I don't want to run. I could have told you that earlier. You're heading south, right? That's exactly where I need to be. It's either *this* . . . or I freeze to death out there. So I think I'll stick with the warm room and the nice car, thanks very much.'

Anton fumbled with the cord. Alyn felt it loosen and exhaled.

He examined the deep pink furrows across his wrists. 'So who put you up to this? Was it her? *Susannah?*'

'Susannah?' Anton frowned. 'I don't know any Susannah.'

'I think you do. The teacher, she practically runs that place . . .'

'I've told you, I don't know her.'

Alyn sighed. *This is going to be harder than I thought.*

'When Pyra found you, she said you were rambling about some girl. A friend of yours?'

Alyn bit his tongue and shrugged. 'I – I was confused, that's all.'

Anton watched his captive with some suspicion. 'And now?'

'Still am,' Alyn conceded truthfully. 'Who do you work for?'

'We're members of a group. We call ourselves the Guild.'

'And what does your group do?'

'We're a training order. You really don't have a clue why you were in that place, right, Alyn?'

Alyn shook his head. 'By now I'm not sure I even care any more,' he said. 'I'm just glad I'm out of there.'

Anton walked over to a table and poured a glass of water from the jug. He gave it to Alyn, who drank it down, spilling most of it on his grey uniform until he erupted into a fit of blustery coughs.

'The people who put you there are our enemies too.'

Convenient, Alyn thought. He couldn't help but feel there might be more to the story than Anton was keen to share. 'Who are they?'

'You know all those crazy government conspiracies you hear about?' said Anton. 'Well, they aren't one of those. From what we know, the Pledge is *more powerful* than the government. I bet the government doesn't have a clue what's going on. Or if they do, they're powerless to stop it.'

Alyn failed to hide his scepticism. 'Really. So there are two secret groups out there: the Pledge and you guys. The Guild.'

'Yup.' Anton chucked him a towel and took the water back.

This stuff doesn't happen in real life, Alyn thought.

'What's that?' Anton said, noticing the folder poking out beneath the zip of Alyn's coat. He snatched the folder and turned through a couple of pages, looking at the names and photographs. 'Where did you find this?'

'In a hut, near the prison. Give it back.'

Anton smiled. 'No chance.'

Defeated, Alyn rested his head back against the carpet.

'This is a list of everyone,' Anton said to himself. He drew a finger along a list of home addresses. 'Of everyone in there. This will come in handy, Alyn. Thank you.'

He stood, tucked the folder under his arm and gave his prisoner a smile as he left the room and locked the door behind him.

9

'Wakey, wakey,' said Julian, watching the sleeping pair.

Harlan and Elsa slowly opened their eyes. After making several changes, the group had been fortunate enough to not encounter any other ticket inspectors until a concerned attendant at the last station approached the group. A fast-thinking Julian declared they were on a school trip to London, had got separated from the rest of their class and were looking for a telephone. When the attendant headed inside to make the call on their behalf, Harlan, Elsa and Julian darted inside the train for the final stretch of their journey.

Harlan had been dozing lightly for the past hour, snatching slivers of sleep every so often and feeling none the better for it. Elsa had passed out for almost the entire journey and was gently snoring. By the time they entered London, the train was filled with passengers.

There was a clattering of bags and the clicking of luggage clasps being fastened as they came to a stop.

Julian climbed to his feet and stepped into the aisle.

Elsa rubbed her eyes and yawned. 'Are we really here?'

'See for yourself,' he said, and gestured to the sign for Euston station outside.

The doors opened and the three shuffled on to the crowded platform, soon engulfed by a swarm of shoving passengers.

Elsa gazed around at the station. The place seemed to pulse with noise. She zipped her hooded coat all the way to her throat, hiding her grey prison uniform beneath.

'It's time we figured out a plan,' said Harlan. 'We're supposed to be waiting for Jes and Ryan –'

'Hold on,' said Julian. '*We?*'

'Yeah. *We.* You're in this with us, whether you like it or not.'

'That doesn't mean I answer to you,' Julian snapped. 'Or you,' he said, poking Elsa's forehead. 'Or anyone.'

'But you can't go it alone,' Elsa said, pushing away his finger. 'We have to stick together; that's why we're waiting for them!'

'I wouldn't hold your breath,' Julian muttered, looking at the trains. 'Not after what I heard in those woods.'

'We'll give it three days,' said Harlan. 'If we've not met up by then, we'll move on. But we can't go home. You know we'll end up putting everyone in danger. That's the first place they'll go looking for us.'

'We could be really careful,' Elsa said. 'I mean, we could sneak home at night and tell our families and –'

Harlan shook his head. 'No, Elsa. Not even if we're careful.'

'*Three days*,' Elsa murmured. It sounded like a long time to be alone without anywhere to sleep. 'What are we going to do? We don't have any money . . .'

Julian made sure no one was watching and showed them a leather wallet. Inside was a wad of notes.

Harlan's eyes widened then settled into a look of disappointment. 'You stole it.'

'It was practically falling out of his pocket.' Julian shrugged. 'If I hadn't taken it, somebody else would.'

'Keep telling yourself that,' Harlan said with a snort. 'Do you have *any* morals?'

'When my belly's full and I have a roof over my head, I have plenty –'

'Lend us something, Julian,' Elsa cut in. 'Just enough for us both to get something to eat. To keep us going. I'm starving!'

'If you want money, you're going to have to find it yourselves.'

'We're not stealing,' Harlan said accusingly.

'Good luck finding a job.' Julian looked at Elsa. 'I'm sure someone's looking for a chimney sweep and at least you're the right size for it . . .'

'You're scum, do you know that, Julian?' Harlan said.

'Why? Because I stole a wallet . . . or because I won't give *you* any of it? Besides, it's not up to me to provide for you. You're going to need to think on your feet – to live by your wits. I'm sure you have *some* between the two of you . . .'

'Julian –'

Julian patted Elsa on the arm and zipped up his coat. 'Meet me back here the same time tomorrow. If not, I'll assume the worst.' He gave them both a nod in parting and followed a man in a suit to the ticket barriers, walking quickly through behind him.

10

Snow was smothering the prison. Groups of children, all in the same grey uniforms and hooded coats, stood in the yard, watching as three guards repaired the fence. A few whispered to one another – *Do you think they really escaped?* – and checked to make sure no guards were listening.

'This silence is a little disconcerting, Claude,' said Susannah, as she and Rayner sat in the infirmary.

Rayner held the gauze against the cut on his forehead. 'They're all innocent,' Rayner said. 'We've kidnapped a hundred children. We're telling them they're criminals, but they aren't. They're innocent.'

'*Innocent*,' she said, pondering. 'A strange word to use, considering your friend is lying dead in a corridor –'

Rayner slammed his fist into the wall with such force that she flinched. 'They didn't do the crimes we were told they had. Correct?'

Susannah nodded. 'Correct.'

'I don't believe it,' Rayner said, caught between a

45

laugh and a growl. 'I don't believe a government could get away with something like this.'

'A government *couldn't* get away with it. Oh, people always think they're involved in these things. The Prime Minister was told – as a matter of courtesy, they claim – but I think the real reason he was told was to show him how powerless he is. Even if he wanted to stop it, he couldn't.'

Rayner snorted. 'Where is he anyway?'

'He's taking an *extended vacation*,' Susannah answered.

'So you're really telling me there's some evil group sitting around plotting everyone's destruction?'

'No, the opposite. There is such a group, but they're concerned about the way the country is going – extremists, anarchists … moral, social and financial ruin. We're no longer a player on the world stage; we're like the fool who forgot his lines. The country is being torn apart at the seams and the Pledge sees this. It's willing to go to lengths that other people wouldn't. If that makes them *evil* …'

'It usually does,' Rayner grumbled. 'Isn't every maniac willing to cross the line?'

'You've seen the recent terrorist attacks. The bomb threats, the violence, the havoc. The Pledge is trying to build a better world, Claude.'

'By using these kids to change the current one? And the kids have got no idea what they're doing, right?'

'That's what the lessons are for. We use subliminal

images of things we want to change. Consciously they don't even see them, but that's the wonderful thing about their Ability. It can be harnessed *unconsciously*. These kids are special, but if they knew what they could do they could become very powerful . . . too powerful.'

Rayner gave no sign he was even listening. 'A better world,' he spat.

'A utopia.'

'A fantasy,' Rayner corrected. 'So who else knows?'

'Just us now,' Susannah replied. 'None of the other guards have any idea either. They're just pawns. And the other ninety-four children in here – they have no idea.'

'Why tell them they're criminals?' Rayner asked. 'What's the point?'

'If we'd just kidnapped them and put them here, they would ask questions. They would resist,' Susannah answered and pointed out of the window to a group of uniformed inmates in the yard. 'We gave them a story, a narrative to fulfil. Memories are easy to manipulate. Everyone needs a part to play. Tell someone they're bad long enough and they start to believe it. It's easier than you think.'

Susannah reached into her pocket and pushed a piece of paper towards Rayner. He snatched it out of her hands.

'It's a recommendation – for you to take Martin Adler's role as chief warden, should anything happen to him –' She paused as Rayner scanned the letter, eyes darting quickly from side to side. 'Regardless, Adler is dead. The job is yours, if you want it, Claude. The prison, the guards ... *the inmates.* You'll have charge of everything. The other arrangements will be left to me.'

Rayner turned his back to her.

'It's what you've always wanted,' she continued. 'To be someone important. To be appreciated. To be respected.'

Rayner watched the snow falling. In the yard, guards were struggling to repair the broken wire-mesh fence.

'There's another group who are helping the prisoners,' Susannah continued. 'I've been aware of their presence for some time now, and their interest in what we're doing. They call themselves the Guild. They're going to try to destroy everything we've worked for. I've tried slowing them down, but I think it might be too late.'

'The man who attacked us – you think he might be part of this group?'

Susannah nodded. 'Yes. As a matter of fact, I know he is.'

Rayner still pressed the gauze against his head. 'I'll get another team back to the forest at once,' he said.

As Rayner left the infirmary, dazed and still in disbelief, the telephone in the office rang. Susannah hesitated, then slowly walked towards it. The phone continued to ring. Eventually she picked it up.

'Yes?' she said quietly, watching as a couple of guards walked along the corridor.

'Ms Dion,' Stephen said. 'I need some updates on the little job you're doing for me regarding Felix's company.'

'Everything's going as planned, Mr Nover,' she said.

'It needs to happen quietly and quickly, as I explained. I need JF Industries to take an almighty hit, but more than that I need him to remain completely unaware.'

'I'm sure he's too busy focusing on other things at the moment,' Susannah said, 'but I'll do what I can.'

Stephen giggled. 'Do, and there is a large bonus with your name on it.'

11

'Wake up,' Henry announced, pushing open the door.

Ryan, who was curled in the corner inside the carapace of a tangled sleeping bag, stirred and nestled deeper into the fabric.

'Five more minutes. Just five more . . .' Ryan's voice trailed off.

'We need to eat,' Henry went on. 'Since you're both my guests for the time being, we're going to need more food. Which means more work.'

Ryan grumbled something, swallowing a mouthful of fabric.

'Are you ill or something?' Henry said.

Still face down in the sleeping bag, Ryan tried shaking his head.

'Good. Because you'll both need to be strong.'

Ryan closed his eyes. 'I am strong,' he mumbled.

'*Fit*,' Henry corrected. 'The forest is enormous. You have any idea how hard it is to trek miles in the snow? The pair of you are weak. You need food. My people will be waiting for you at the edge of the forest. But first you need to *get* there.'

'Yeah, whatever. Just five more minutes . . .'

Henry marched over to him and tore the zip down. 'Welcome to the real world, Ryan,' he said. 'Now get up.'

Ryan rolled over, his forearm over his eyes. 'You're even worse than the damned guards . . .'

He reluctantly sat up, nursing his head, and looked at Jes, who was dozing peacefully on a sleeping bag. Ryan slipped into his coat and followed Henry into the tunnel and up the ladder.

'So where are we supposed to find food?' he said as they reached the top, shivering.

'I have some traps,' Henry said. 'But we'll need to be careful. There are probably still guards out there, looking for you.'

Henry nodded, then noticed Ryan's coat. 'Is that an ibis?'

Ryan looked down at the ibis. He had picked it up just after they left with Jes, but he hadn't given it much thought until now. 'Took it from one of the guards. You seen one before or something?'

'I'd heard rumours of this sort of weaponry being developed. Always thought they were just stories, though.' He examined the weapon cautiously and handed it back to Ryan. 'Keep it safe. You never know when we'll need it.'

The pair walked slowly, not speaking much other

than Henry telling Ryan to watch for the occasional dip or branch. They were almost a mile into the forest when Ryan paused, light-headed and breathless.

'You need to eat,' Henry said. 'The traps aren't far. We'll be there soon.'

A quarter of an hour later the pair found Henry's first trap, containing a wriggling hare, scrambling at the snow.

'If you're squeamish, you might want to look away.'

'I'm not squeamish.'

Henry quickly snapped the animal's neck and brushed a layer of snow away from its fur with his sleeve.

'We can cook this back in the tunnel. If we light a fire here, it might alert the guards. Jes needs to eat.'

'You reckon she'll be all right then? I mean with the wound and everything . . .'

Henry turned the animal over in his hands. 'People have survived much worse. The bullet is out, and the wound is clean. And I've got enough painkillers, for a few more days, anyway. So do you go to school, Ryan?'

'*Did*. Before this.'

'How did you find it?'

'Hated it. Couldn't wait to get out of there. You're gonna tell me it's the best days of my life, I'll bet –'

'No,' said Henry with a smile. 'As a matter of fact I never liked school much either.'

Ryan nodded and sank his elbows on to his knees, looking around at the trees, half expecting to see signs of movement.

'I don't know why you're sitting down,' Henry went on. 'I'll need some help collecting wood for the fire. Fetch some branches. Big ones.'

Ryan grudgingly stood and gathered some branches from the snow, sighing with each swoop.

'Why don't you tell me some more about "Nowhere", Ryan?'

Ryan wiped a foam of snow away from a branch with his sleeve. 'Nothing to tell. Everyone there is just a bloody actor.'

'What exactly did they have you doing in there?'

'Chores. Work. Those stupid lessons we told you about. There was a woman – she said she was a teacher and she wanted to help us, but she was just another liar.'

Ryan looked down at the faint lines on his hand left by the papercuts Susannah had forced Jes to give him.

'Soon as Jes is better, we're out of here – as far away from Nowhere as possible,' Ryan muttered. 'We're going after them.'

Henry threw another branch on to the pile, shaking his head. 'You're angry. I understand that.'

You don't know the half of it, Ryan snarled inwardly, feeling himself getting worked up. He drove his forearm across a branch, splitting it in two, and gathered up the broken pieces, chucking them with the others.

'The Guild will be on the way,' Henry said. 'They'll make sure you're looked after.'

'They gonna help us go after this Pledge?' Ryan said.

'They'll make sure you're looked after,' Henry said evasively. He patted Ryan on the arm. 'Come on. Let's go back and get this cooked. You must be hungry.'

12

Pyra launched a bundle of clothes at a sleeping Alyn.

'You've got five minutes to get out of your uniform – you still look like a prisoner. Then we're leaving.'

Alyn wiped his eyes. His cheek was mottled with the imprint from the cheap carpet fibres and felt numb.

'Not used to getting up when you're told?' taunted Pyra.

'Not used to changing in front of random women,' Alyn clarified, climbing cautiously to his feet.

Pyra sighed and turned her back. Alyn pulled off the stained, sweat- and snow-drenched grey uniform and tossed it into the bin in the corner of the room. *Glad I never have to wear that thing again*, he thought.

He stepped clumsily into the jeans, yanked the T-shirt down over his head and slipped his arms into the leather jacket.

'Can I trust you to walk to the car, Alyn?' Pyra said.

'Yeah. I'll walk.'

Pyra picked up a rucksack from the table, hoisted it over her shoulder and left the room, pulling Alyn along by the forearm. He took a final look at the television in the corner of the room, which showed a suburban street in the aftermath of a riot.

The three quickly left the hotel and marched across the gravel to the car.

Pyra opened the rear door. 'Go on,' she said. 'Get in.'

'You two should have your own show,' Alyn said, ducking underneath her arm. '*The Travelling Kidnappers* –'

'We're not kidnappers.'

'Yeah? Then why do I feel like I'm your prisoner?'

'Cos you're used to being one,' Pyra answered as the car pulled away. 'It's all you've known in that place. You probably aren't used to trusting people.'

'And, unless you want to end up getting caught, you'll need to trust us,' Anton said, and put the silver taser down the side of his seat.

Alyn said nothing and folded his arms. Through the car window he watched as a flock of migrating birds zigzagged fluidly and nimbly across the desolate white sky.

'So what now? You're going after the Pledge, right?'

'We would,' said Pyra. 'If we knew who they were.'

'Or what they are doing?'

'We know what they're doing.' Pyra looked back at him. 'They were manipulating all of you. Harnessing something you have.'

Alyn looked to Anton's eyes in the rear-view mirror, hoping he might explain.

'You have a gift, Alyn,' he said. 'Like us. That's what we – the Guild – are. We're a training order. We'll teach you how to use it.'

Even more baffled, Alyn turned back to Pyra.

'Have you ever noticed yourself surrounded by coincidences?' Pyra asked.

'I'm finding myself surrounded by crazy people, if that counts.'

Anton turned down a deserted lane, only to find the road blocked.

'The police yesterday, and now this? Seems like someone's determined to slow us down,' Pyra said.

'So you're saying we –'

'Hold on a minute,' Anton said, silencing Alyn. A second car emerged from the trees and parked across the tarmac, trapping them.

'We're surrounded,' Pyra whispered. 'Alyn, keep low. They're looking for you.'

'Keep low?'

'Just *do it*!'

A stocky man stepped out of the car in front. He was wearing fingerless gloves and a military-style coat.

Anton glanced in the mirror. Another man, dressed similarly, came out of the car behind and leant against its bonnet with his arms folded. He smiled at the trio.

Pyra leant out of the window. 'Why are you blocking the road? Who are you?'

The man sauntered towards them. 'Just a quick check that you ain't hiding anything. Then you can go.'

Alyn pressed closer to the floor. It was hard to hear anything.

'We're not hiding anything, pal. We're in a rush,' said Anton. 'We have somewhere to be.'

'Oh?'

'We really have to get going. Can you please move your car . . . ?'

'Soon,' the man said. 'Just a quick check, like I said.'

He walked round to the driver's seat and peered into the back.

Alyn jumped so much that he caught the back of his head on the seat.

The man stood up straight, smiling. 'Well, well. You do realize there's someone in the back of your car?'

'Yeah. He's my little brother,' Pyra replied.

'Why's he on the floor?'

'Because he's an idiot. Like most teenagers. We good to go?'

The man put his hand on the roof of the car and lowered down. 'No chance.'

'Guess he's got us.' Anton looked at Pyra. 'I'll go first.'

He obediently unbuckled his seatbelt, then reached for the door handle. Anton closed his eyes and murmured something quickly under his breath. Just as the man was about to reach inside, a tiny, almost insignificant fly was blown off its course and collided with his eyelash. The man flinched, in which time Anton grabbed the door handle and slammed the car door against his forehead.

The man fell back, stunned, and landed on one knee.

Anton hopped outside and dodged an oncoming punch from his ally.

Alyn scrambled up, eyes wide, to witness Pyra vault across the bonnet and deliver a kick to the side of his head.

Anton blocked a second punch with his forearm, and whirled round, elbowing his attacker in the side of the face.

The man fell to the ground, dazed, as Anton spun in the opposite direction and threw another elbow into his mouth.

Alyn winced at the cracking sound, and the sight of their slumped attacker fumbling with a mouthful of broken teeth.

The pair darted back inside the car. Anton slammed his foot on to the accelerator and steered the car on to the grass.

Alyn looked out of the back window at the two fallen men; one was barely conscious, the other was trying to rise unsteadily to his knees.

'That stuff I was saying about being surrounded by crazy people,' Alyn said, wide-eyed, as the car tore down the lane. 'Just so you know ... I was kidding.'

13

It was almost ten o'clock at night. Elsa and Harlan had been sitting against the station wall in silence for the past few hours, enviously watching the shuffling queues in the food court.

Elsa wrapped her arms round her groaning stomach. 'Can't we find somewhere else to sit, Harlan? It's like we're torturing ourselves ...'

Harlan shook his head. 'We've got a clear view of the platform. If Jes and Ryan took the train, we'll spot them straight away. Or they'll see us. That's why we're here, remember?'

'Hope you're right,' she mumbled, burying her mouth inside the coat. She watched enviously as a young girl walked past devouring a burger, licking the spilled sauce from her fingers.

'*I am*. But you know who else is right, Elsa? Julian. We have to adapt.'

'But then we'll be just as bad as they say we are ...'

'They haven't left us with much choice, have they?'

As he said this, a passing man tossed a couple of coins on to the floor in front of them.

Elsa clawed the money towards her. 'A pound!' she said excitedly. 'We can use this to call our parents, Harlan. I don't care what the others said. We can't do this by ourselves. We have to call them. They could come and get us. I swear we'd be all right –'

Harlan closed his eyes. 'We've already talked about this. Do you really want to put them in danger?'

'What about *us*?' she cried, with tears in her eyes. 'We're already in danger. I'm tired and hungry. I want to go home!'

Harlan patted Elsa's shoulders sympathetically and got to his feet.

Elsa went to stand. 'Where are you going? I don't want to stay here by myself . . .'

Harlan struggled with a smile. 'Just wait here for me.'

Harlan rested his forearms on a railing across the road from the station. The closest he had come was stopping someone to ask for the time. But even then he'd lifted his hand leadenly and froze. As he slunk away, Harlan accepted, with some regret, that he lacked the fluency of touch that seemed to come so easily to pickpockets and thieves.

'Hey.'

Harlan started. 'Elsa. I thought I told you to wait for me in the station?'

Elsa wrapped her arms round her chest and backed against the railing. 'I wasn't gonna stay there by myself. What are you doing?'

'Nothing,' he replied, lowering his eyes. 'Just ... waiting.'

'You were going to steal from someone,' Elsa said. 'Like Julian.'

Harlan cradled the base of his neck. 'I can't do it, Elsa. There must be some other way ...'

'There's not,' she said. 'Unless we cook a pigeon or something. And that may not be such a bad idea.' Eyeing a nearby pigeon, Elsa started tiptoeing slowly towards it. 'Here, pigeon, pigeon,' she cooed.

Elsa leant down and dived for it. The bird jerked its neck and flew some way away. It landed on a shop awning and crooked its neck at her with a look of intense curiosity.

'At least I was trying!' she snapped. 'Maybe Julian was right about not waiting for the others.' Elsa scuffed her boot on the pavement. 'I mean, what are the chances we'll find them anyway? What if they hitch-hiked? What if they're not even coming? What if they're *dead*? We might never see them again and before we know it, someone else might get to *us* first.'

Harlan turned away and nodded.

'You're not supposed to agree!' she exclaimed, pushing him. 'You're supposed to tell me everything's going to be all right, that we're going to go back inside and they'll be waiting for us, and we'll find the Pledge and all the answers and then we'll go home! *That's* what you're supposed to say!'

Harlan held a weak smile. 'For now we need food. And shelter. We need *money*. And there's only one way to get money and . . . and I just can't do it.'

Elsa watched a man walk past them and paused. 'Maybe *I* could.'

The pair looked as the man nonchalantly shoved a wallet into the back of his trousers, waddling briskly along the pavement.

'Wait here,' Elsa whispered, gesturing to an alleyway.

Harlan slipped to the side, watching her from behind the wall.

Elsa quickened her pace, checking she had not gained anyone's suspicion, and fell in rhythm with the man's feet, moving lightly, almost cat-like in his shadow. Over on the next road a group of musicians were performing outside a shuttered shop. In the middle of them, a wiry man with tattoos creeping up his neck was sitting on the pavement, ecstatically slamming a tribal drum.

Spurred on by the steady slam of the tribal drum, Elsa extended her hand, her eyes fixed on the bulging wallet.

Take it, she commanded herself. *He'll never even notice.*

Her hand moved closer, fingers poised. The closer she was, the louder the drumming and singing seemed. Elsa looked back over her shoulder, but there was no sign of Harlan.

She reached further, and at that moment there was a

sudden splitting sound and the pounding ceased. The tattooed man's sweating hand had broken through the skin of the tribal drum. The rest of the musicians abruptly stopped and the gathered onlookers cheered ironically.

Elsa's target stopped and turned his head in the direction of the commotion. Elsa dipped forward, swiped the wallet swiftly and gathered it to her chest. *I've got it!*

She turned, about to sprint back to Harlan, when she felt a firm hand on her shoulder.

'I believe that's *mine*,' said the man, looming over her. He snatched the wallet out of her hand. 'Police!'

He tried to grab her with his other hand, but Elsa moved out of the way just in time.

'Run!' she yelled, running to where Harlan was waiting. '*Run!*'

14

Julian turned the key in the hotel-room door and coiled inside like smoke.

Without removing his coat, he flopped backwards on to the bed, arms outstretched until his fingers dangled limply over the sides. The sound of traffic hummed through the window as he watched the ceiling fan whirling, throwing shapes and shadows over him.

Julian gave an irritated grunt. The room was already chilly enough. He climbed wearily off the bed and tugged at the pull string, but still the fan whirred above him.

He yanked it again harder and the pull string snapped in his hand.

Julian was about to call down to the reception to report the broken fan, but paused, thinking better of it. *Don't want to draw unnecessary attention to myself.*

It was good fortune that he hadn't been asked for identification upon paying for his room; the attendant had given him a suspicious look, but said nothing and gladly accepted his money.

Julian emptied his coat pockets, examining the black cylinder of the ibis and the stolen wallet. There was probably enough money to last a few days – perhaps a week. Enough time for him to make a good start on investigating his captors. Julian hid the wallet behind the table, the ibis beneath the bed and turned his eyes to the window.

Across the road was the station. His thoughts drifted to Elsa and Harlan; he imagined them cold and hungry, begging for food.

'Sympathy is overrated,' he declared, shivering on his side under the blanket.

15

'Good morning, I'm here to see Antonia,' Felix said to the bemused housekeeper. 'May I?'

The housekeeper looked behind her, then nodded, quickly stepping aside. Felix smiled, beating his damp hat against his coat, and walked into the hall.

'James,' Antonia said from the staircase. 'Is something the matter?'

'Something has come up,' he said. He turned to the housekeeper, who, interpreting his glance as a command to disappear, scurried back along the hallway.

'Come,' Antonia said.

Felix followed all five feet of her up the stairs and on to the landing.

A girl, not much more than four years old, appeared from one of the rooms, dragging a doll along behind her. She looked up at Felix and waved coyly.

'This must be Sophia,' he said, kneeling down. 'I've heard a lot about you.'

The girl looked at Felix, a little puzzled, and offered him her doll.

'This way, James,' said Antonia. She glared at her adopted daughter and as soon as Felix was in tow walked through to a room with large double windows.

Antonia lowered herself into a seat. Her black bob shone in the morning light.

'Stephen's wealth is increasing,' Felix said. 'Rapidly. I think it would be a good idea if he were removed from the Pledge before he overtakes me. And takes charge.'

Antonia raised a bejewelled hand. 'No, James. Perhaps some fresh blood is what we need.'

'And blood you will get, with him in charge,' Felix quipped. 'The project will be in his hands, more or less. You trust him to hold that much power?'

'James,' Antonia said. 'I don't trust *anyone* with that much power. But if the power comes to Stephen, all we can do is offer our support. And guidance . . . just like we agreed all those years ago when we formed.'

Felix waited a moment before speaking. 'They've still not been found. Which means . . .'

'They'll be here,' Antonia murmured. 'Looking for us. If they aren't already.'

'No, looking for *me*,' Felix answered. 'They found me on Susannah's phone, remember? I've tried to play things down in front of the rest of the Pledge, but –'

'You're worried.'

'Yes,' Felix said. 'I'm worried. We took so many precautions, Antonia. The prison, the guards, the forest . . . I was sure the project would reach its conclusion without a hitch.' Felix shook his head sadly.

'Maybe we were fools to think the project could have ever really worked, James.'

'It's too late for that,' Felix said. 'But do tell me if you ever change your mind about Stephen, won't you?'

Antonia smiled. 'The only chance of me changing my mind is if you use their Ability to change it for me.'

Felix gave a brief smile in return, thinking about what she'd said. 'I'll see myself out,' he said.

16

Jes slowly sat up straight and pivoted, letting her legs dangle from the table. Gently, she lowered her feet to the floor and limped, hunched over, to the door. She pushed it aside.

The tunnel corridor was similar – virtually identical – to the one where she had killed Adler. She touched the wall and let her fingers explore the cold stone.

She continued walking some way until she came across a dark puddle.

Jes peered down, lowering to her knees. Her face was a pale, slight reflection in the liquid. She placed her hand in the puddle, stroking her reflection. '*I'm sorry,*' she murmured as her tears disturbed the dark water, remembering back to the night of the escape and how she'd fired at the chief warden, again and again, wishing him dead. The anger had felt like a black weight in her chest.

When she opened her eyes, she thought for a moment that Adler's face was staring back at her.

There was a noise from the end of the corridor and Ryan appeared on the ladder. Jes got to her feet slowly.

'All right,' Ryan said, grinning at her. 'Came to see you earlier but you were still asleep.'

He proudly handed her a piece of charred meat. 'We made a fire in the ladder shaft. Had to wait until dark or the guards would've seen the smoke. Still, better late than never, right?'

'You caught this yourself?' asked Jes, turning it over in her hands.

'Yup.'

Jes looked at him quizzically. 'Really?'

'Well, it was Henry's trap. I just helped build the fire. But I built a damn good fire.'

Jes brought the meat close to her mouth and took a cautious bite, and before she had even finished chewing, a second, then a third.

Before long the meat had vanished, and Jes was eyeing Ryan in the hope that he had brought more.

'That's all we got,' he said apologetically.

'Next time I'll come with you,' she said with a smile. 'I'll get my own food.'

'Not for a while, you won't.' He nodded towards her wound.

'I'm fine,' she said, and tried to stand up straight, but quickly withdrew into a stoop.

Ryan reached out to support her. 'Henry said we have to stay until you're better.'

'I don't want to stay. I just want to get out of here as soon as possible,' she said. 'I want to find the others. I want –' she paused, gesturing to the surrounding darkness – '*light*.'

She was cut short as the lid was sealed and Henry began climbing down. 'How are you feeling?' he asked Jes once he reached the bottom.

'Better after the food. Ryan told me he built a fire.'

Henry laughed. 'Ryan couldn't build a fire in a room full of matches. He put ours out about three times.'

'Oi! I wasn't that bad,' Ryan said, glaring at Henry. He turned to Jes. 'It's just because it was cold and wet . . .'

'I thought every boy knew how to make a fire.'

'Yeah, maybe in *your* day they could,' Ryan said. 'Do I look like I was in the Scouts?' He began to walk away.

Henry turned to Jes. 'Now that you're awake, I think you – and Ryan – need to know exactly what's going on.'

Ryan stopped in his tracks and looked back over his shoulder.

'I think you both need to know why you were taken,' Henry added.

'All of you in the prison have one thing in common,' Henry explained, as the pair huddled together close to him. The flickering candle flame danced with his words. 'You can make things happen – things that might seem highly unlikely. And you're not the only ones. There's a whole community of people – *the Guild* – people just like you ... people who have been training for years, developing the Ability ... learning how to manipulate and influence reality.'

'Eh?' Ryan said after several seconds of silence.

Henry tapped the side of his incredulous guest's head. 'Somewhere in here are all your thoughts, fears and desires ... and your *imagination*. Somehow, through a string of highly improbable coincidences, you can use that imagination to make things in here –' he tapped Ryan's head again – 'happen out *here*. In the real world.'

Ryan felt himself getting a headache already. 'You mean like –'

'Magic.' Jes finished his sentence, not taking her eyes off the flickering flame.

'I wouldn't call it magic,' Henry said. 'It seems to work through coincidence and chance and probability.'

Ryan yawned and rubbed his eyes with his forearm. He glanced at Jes, who seemed to be following Henry's baffling claims.

'If this is true, and I'm not even sure I believe it myself,' she said, 'then it still doesn't explain why they've put us through all of this ...' Jes pointed at her prison uniform. 'Why put us in that place? Why all the lies?'

'This skill is far, far rarer in adults than it is young people. Individually you can make small things happen. But with a hundred of you, all together, you can change reality on a massive scale. What kind of changes, we don't know ... but if the members of the Pledge are the kind of people who kidnap children and teenagers from their homes, I can only imagine –'

'Look, no offence, mate,' Ryan said with a laugh, 'but it sounds like the kinda thing Harlan would be well into, but me? Nah.'

'You have to realize how bizarre it sounds,' Jes agreed.

'You want proof?' Henry said, looking at the pair. 'Put out the flame.'

'Easy,' Ryan said, and inhaled a mouthful of breath.

Henry put up his hand. 'Not like that.'

Jes shut her eyes and tried willing the flame to extinguish. But when she opened them it was still swaying gently.

'When was the last time wishing worked for you? Use your *imagination*. When you get it right, you'll feel something change in your mind.'

'You think putting out some candle is gonna prove anything?'

'If you can do this,' Henry said, and pointed at the candle, 'you can do anything.'

He slowly got to his feet and walked over to the door.

'Wait, where are you going?'

'You don't need me here. I don't have the Ability. The two of you need to try together, without any distractions.'

He left the pair with the flame serenely descending the candle.

'I still think he's nuts,' Ryan grumbled. 'You know

74

what I was doing the night they took me?' Ryan went on. 'We were taking my best friend's dad's car out for a ride.'

'I was at a party,' Jes said quietly, still staring at the flame. 'They must've been following me for ages. Waiting for the right moment.'

'You didn't strike me as the sort – to be out partying, I mean. Thought you were a good girl.' He paused. 'Here's where you're supposed to say you were surprised about me – that I didn't seem like the sort either.'

'Well, you do.'

'Cheers,' he said sarcastically. 'You're a rich girl, aren't you? Bet you had piano lessons and everything.'

'My parents are wealthy enough, I guess,' she said.

Ryan snorted. 'Mum barely makes enough to get by. That's why I'm getting a job as soon as I finish school.'

'What kind of job?'

'Dunno. Anything. I don't care, me.'

Jes looked concerned. 'Isn't there anything you want to do?'

'Who knows. I'll just take it as it comes. It's no biggie.'

'My dad says you have to take control of your own life, or someone else will.'

'What happens when you don't have a choice?' he asked. 'Now we're down here, can I ask you something?' He waited for Jes to nod permission and said, 'If things were different, you know with our situation and everything, would you . . .' He stopped, noticing Jes was studying him intently. 'Like, if I was at that party with

75

you and your mates . . . do you think you could see us being friends?'

'Sure. I guess so.'

'What about . . .' He trailed off. 'You know.'

'Nope. You've lost me.'

'Hooking up?'

'*Hooking up?*' Jes made no attempt to hide her disdain at the expression.

'Yeah, you know, like –'

'I know what it means.' She looked away. 'I'm sorry, Ryan. I like you as a friend, but . . .'

'But?'

'But that's it. You're not really – how can I put this . . . ?'

'It's all right,' he said with a shrug. 'You don't need to say anything else.'

'Sorry.'

'Nah, it's cool. It's not like I fancy you or anything. I was just wondering.' He grinned sheepishly. 'Something to pass the time, you know.'

With his cheeks burning, Ryan turned his eyes to the candle, desperately willing the darkness to swallow him. He imagined the soft hiss as the flame suddenly extinguished, and the smoky-sweet scent of blown-out birthday candles. Ryan felt a tingling sensation in the middle of his forehead, a little like pins and needles. At that moment a single drop of condensation slithered free from a crack in the stone ceiling and landed straight on the candle.

76

The room fell into darkness except for a winding grey thread of smoke.

'That's it,' said an excited Henry, opening the door.

'Oi, were you spying on us?' Ryan complained.

'I knew you could do it.' Henry grinned and lit a match, making his way across the room. 'Do you believe me now? Do you understand?'

'Yeah, but it wasn't us,' Ryan said, shrugging. 'It was just a drop of water.'

'It was a coincidence,' Jes agreed.

Henry leant down to light the candle. 'That's how the Ability works. It causes a chain reaction of unlikely events, one after the other.' Henry's eyes were filled with excitement. 'Now do it again.'

17

His head pulsing from so long on the motorway, Alyn sat up and rubbed his eyes to see snowflakes tumbling gently all around the car.

'You can get out and stretch your legs while we fill up the car,' said Pyra. 'But if you even think about trying anything . . .'

'No chance. I've seen what happens to people who annoy you. Anyway, I'm looking forward to meeting this Guild you guys have told me about. And then going after the Pledge, or whatever they're called . . .'

Pyra laughed. '*You* won't be going after the Pledge, Alyn. You'd get yourself killed.'

'Then why are *you*?'

'Because we're trained,' Anton said, chipping in. 'You'll be able to join us as soon as we've trained you, but until then . . .'

'The Pledge put me in that place,' Alyn seethed. 'They put us all through this. And now you're telling me I can't do anything?'

'Don't look too annoyed, Alyn,' Anton said. 'We're not exactly looking forward to it.'

'Whatever. Anyway, I need the toilet,' Alyn said, and unbuckled his seatbelt.

Anton looked at Pyra. 'You stay here. I'll take him.'

'Take me? You really think I'm going to run? I've got a cosy ride home . . .'

'Home? You ain't going home, Alyn. You're with *us* now.'

They got out of the car and Anton shoved him in the small of the back towards the services. Alyn trotted forward and sank his hands into his pockets. 'Can I have some money, then?'

'For what?'

'Sweets.'

'*Sweets?*' Anton rolled his eyes and wearily slapped some change into Alyn's hand. 'Bloody kids.'

The electric doors parted and Alyn stepped inside, followed by Anton. The door to the toilet was over on the far wall, beside an assortment of car accessories: ice scrapers, air fresheners and ornaments.

'Be quick.'

Alyn nodded, pushed through the door and stepped inside.

He locked the cubicle door behind him, lowered the toilet seat and stood on it, fiddling with the clasps of the window above. When there was a gap just large enough, Alyn pulled himself up and squeezed through.

I'm not with you, Alyn thought as he landed on a couple of black bags outside. *I'm on my own. And I'm going to find the Pledge whether you like it or not.*

18

'I see someone's been taking pity on you.' Julian smirked, kneeling beside a miserable-looking Harlan and Elsa. The pair were sitting in a little alcove, a short way from the main platforms. He nodded to the few scattered pennies. '*Pity*,' he went on. 'What an awful word that is! It just forces itself from the lips; you practically have to spit it . . .'

'Get lost, Julian.' Elsa turned away from him and closed her eyes.

How had he *found it so easy to steal?* Elsa regretfully accepted that other than being cunning, smug and treacherous, Julian was that most useful of traits: adaptable. She remembered learning about survival of the fittest in school, with the class rat shown to them as an example of such an attribute. In her mind's eye, the rat's pointy little features slowly transformed to Julian's.

'We're twenty-five pence off a sandwich,' Harlan said.

Julian shook his head. 'Cruel to be kind, et cetera, et cetera. Someday you'll understand.'

As Julian said this, Elsa caught sight of a wad of money nestled inside his coat pocket. *Keep him talking, Harlan*, she thought, gradually bringing her hand up and pretending to scratch her neck.

'You're going to let us starve?' Harlan pleaded. 'Elsa's only a kid, Julian. How can you –'

'I'm not going to tell you again,' Julian hissed, getting to his feet. '*I* look after number one – that's me, if you hadn't guessed. You're wasting your time waiting for Jes and Ryan. They aren't coming! If I were you, I'd find somewhere else to stay.'

'Wait,' Elsa said, her hand hovering mid-air. 'Where are you going?'

'I'm going to start looking for some answers,' he replied. 'By myself.'

With that, he turned and merged with the hurrying crowd.

Harlan carefully manoeuvred into a sitting position. He closed his eyes and tilted his neck back.

'We need to go back out, Elsa.' His head sagged. 'We have to keep trying. The others will be here soon. We'll find them and then everything will be OK . . .'

'Harlan,' Elsa said, nudging him.

Harlan slowly opened his eyes. In Elsa's hand was Julian's wad of stolen money.

'Never thought I'd say this,' Harlan murmured contentedly. 'But I couldn't eat another thing . . .'

He slunk deeper into the metal chair and tiredly

examined the few solitary pizza crusts in the grease-stained cardboard box.

Elsa, who was sprawled beside him, groaned. 'Tell me about it. That pizza was bigger than me . . .'

'Not hard.'

Elsa nudged him with her elbow. 'Shut up and pass me the drink.'

Harlan lazily reached over and pushed a large cup of Coca-Cola towards her.

'I don't fancy being around when Julian realizes his money's gone,' she said, grabbing it.

Harlan smiled, imagining a flustered and irate Julian. 'I can't think of anything better.'

19

After his escape from Pyra and Anton, Alyn walked into the late afternoon, not knowing where he was.

Before long he reached a motorway underpass daubed with erratic graffiti. A snow-covered sign for Leicester loomed over him, indicating that London was still eighty-five miles away. Some empty bottles and polystyrene cups were strewn across the concrete slope and puddles, and wrappers and plastic bags had accumulated in a little nest.

Alyn ventured along the incline, treading down clumps of weeds that were poking through the stone. He stamped down a bush and curled into a foetal position. Although it was too cold to stay long, the sides of the underpass were enough to shield him from the lashing winds, roaring at his face.

If I sleep now, I can walk through the night, he thought.

He waited, eyes closed, and snuggled deeper into his jacket.

*

As a lorry thundered by, Alyn awoke, shivering. The scent of smoke and oil seemed to hover in the air, and he coughed, spluttering.

Maybe I should've stuck with those two weirdos, Alyn considered sleepily, staring at the rattling traffic. Then again, they'd said that going after the people responsible was strictly forbidden, and there was no way he could ever agree to that. *If only I had something to go on.*

'Give me a clue,' Alyn said aloud, looking towards the sky. 'Anything! Let me know who's behind it all!'

It was not so much a prayer as an order.

With a tingling sensation in the back of his mind that he attributed to fatigue, Alyn climbed clumsily out of the foliage and stumbled to a metal barrier. He walked for a few minutes with not even a thought in his mind to accompany him, when a car flew past, sending a muddied newspaper flapping into his face.

Alyn cursed and peeled the wet newspaper away. He was about to throw it into the undergrowth at the side of the motorway when he spotted the words:

HIDDEN CONNECTIONS?

Beneath was a photograph of an amiable-looking white-haired man with heavy-lidded blue eyes and glasses.

'James ... Felix,' Alyn read the caption aloud, straightening the page.

A car whizzed past, making the newspaper flutter in

his hands. Alyn held it firm and stared at the rippling image.

It's him, Alyn realized, as a chain of memories suddenly joined together. *He was there the night I was taken.*

Alyn lowered himself against the barrier, squinting at the sagging paper.

> It is not the first time that the sixty-five-year-old billionaire has come under fire. Protestors last year staged a demonstration outside Pillar, home to Felix's offices, as a response to his company's continuing tax avoidance . . .

'Pillar,' Alyn muttered and looked at the photo below, depicting the glass skyscraper towering over its neighbours.

That's where I need to go, he thought, folding the paper and shoving it inside his pocket.

20

'Here,' Henry said, and tossed the lifeless hare towards Ryan, who moved out of the way.

Jes leant down and picked up the animal. The harsh white of the snow burned into her eyes.

'You OK carrying that thing?' Ryan said, with a look of disgust.

Jes nodded, gazing at the floppy animal in her hands.

Ryan waited until Henry was out of earshot before saying, 'It still don't make any sense,' he spat. 'And I *still* think the old man's crazy.'

'Have you got a better explanation?' Jes said serenely, lowering the hare.

'Whoa, hang on. Don't tell me you're even considering it . . .'

'Ever since they took us it feels like we stepped into the looking-glass.'

'Eh?'

'Alice in Wonderland,' she said. 'Never mind. You know, Ryan, my friends always said I was really lucky.

Like I always landed on my feet, no matter what. Maybe this whole time it was this Ability thing.'

'You got *shot*.'

'But I *survived*.'

The pair stopped walking as Henry halted and raised his arm. 'Guards,' he hissed. 'Two of them. Both of you get back.'

Henry retreated slowly, his eyes fixed on the men, two black shapes in the trees.

Ryan trod back up a ridge of snow and held his hand out for Jes to take. 'Down here,' he said, pulling her back towards the stream. 'The tunnel is just over this way.'

The pair hurried to the cover. Ryan kicked the snow aside and pulled the lid away. He gestured for Jes to go first.

Jes knelt and lowered herself on to the ladder. Ryan waited until she was a few metres below and went in after her. He soon reached the bottom, where Jes was leaning against the wall, clutching her side.

'Guess that was a bit ambitious,' she said, forcing a smile.

'Here,' Ryan said. 'Let me check.' He moved closer to her and lifted up her cut uniform. His fingers fell on skin. Jes gasped with how cold they felt. 'Sorry,' he laughed.

He looked at the dressing. 'Looks OK still. I mean, it's not reopened.' The ladder at the end of the corridor began to rattle. 'That sounds like Henry.'

'You can take your hand away now,' Jes said.

Ryan's cold face seemed to burn. He released Jes's uniform and dusted the snow crystals from her coat as Henry emerged back in the tunnel.

'Give me the hare,' he said. 'We'll have to wait until later to cook it. I'll find somewhere to store it for now.'

Jes passed him the animal. 'Henry,' she said before he had a chance to turn away, 'I just wanted to thank you for everything you've done. For saving me – us – from the guards. For letting us stay here.'

'It's no problem.' He went to walk away but Jes stopped him.

'We really mean it,' she continued. 'Who knows where we'd be if it weren't for you. But, we have to meet our friends.'

'The others,' Ryan clarified. 'We were supposed to meet them down in London.'

'So if it's OK with you, we'll be on our way,' Jes added, 'first thing tomorrow.'

Henry seemed taken aback and Jes thought for a moment that she might have offended him.

'I can't let you leave,' he said, shaking his head.

'Hey, hang on a minute,' Ryan said.

'No,' Henry said firmly. 'You saw what happened just now, didn't you? The forest is still being patrolled.' He turned to Jes. 'And you can't even run with your wound. What chance have you got? *None*.'

'The Ability,' Jes said.

'You don't know how to use it. Which is why I've arranged for the Guild to come and collect you.'

'What about the other kids in the prison? Who's coming to save them?'

'I'm figuring that out,' Henry said. 'That's why I'm here.'

'So this *Guild* is coming to rescue us?' Jes confirmed, to make sure she understood.

'But we don't need rescuing!' Ryan said, frustrated.

Henry looked at him. 'You really think so, Ryan?'

'Yeah, I do actually. Where were *your* lot when we needed them? Where were they when we were stuck in that dump, with nutters trying to brainwash us? They weren't anywhere. We did it all ourselves. No one helped us. *No one!*'

Henry opened his mouth to answer him, but Ryan had already walked away.

21

It was late afternoon inside the train station. Crowds of passengers were breezing past Harlan and Elsa, mostly oblivious to the pair of ragged teenagers on the metal bench. If anything, it was the stench of their unwashed clothes that attracted the most attention from passers-by, who avoided their eyes out of fear that they might be expected to part with their spare change.

'Here,' Elsa said, stealthily passing a small cylinder of notes held with an elastic band to Harlan. 'I think we should each keep half. Just in case . . .'

'In case?'

'Something happens to one of us.' She looked around carefully. 'Can I tell you something?'

'Sure.'

'I think we're being watched.' *I know we're being watched*, she thought, peering at a couple of men stood by a bench.

'Watched? By who?'

'I dunno exactly. But I've seen people looking at us.

And not just regular looking. I mean *looking*. I don't think we should stay.'

'You're paranoid, Elsa. It's probably the lack of sleep. No one even knows we're here.'

'Well, I think we need to get out of here,' Elsa said, unconvinced.

'We need to give Jes and Ryan some more time to find us,' Harlan replied, slipping the money inside his coat.

'We can't wait any more,' Elsa argued. 'We were better off back at the prison.' *At least we had a bed*.

She wearily watched the swarming passengers moving incessantly in great floods.

'Hey, I'll look after you,' Harlan said. He put his arm across her shoulders. 'I promise.'

Elsa tried to smile. She looked at the display board, watching helplessly as the letters and numbers slid past. She wished she could confess to Harlan her desire to leave, to get aboard the next train home, but it was hopeless. She knew what he'd say, scolding her. Who did he think he was, her brother? Elsa only had one brother, and he was waiting for her at home.

'Cheer up,' Harlan said, playfully jabbing her side, as though reading her mind. 'At least things won't be as bad as before.'

'I guess,' Elsa said. She wiped her face with her hands to keep herself awake. 'I'm thirsty. I'm going to get a drink.'

With that, Elsa scurried into the crowd of passing commuters.

'I bet you think you're clever,' came a voice from behind Harlan. He felt something pressing into his back.

Julian stepped round to the front. The ibis was tucked into his sleeve.

Harlan shrugged, standing up. 'I only have half. Elsa has the rest.'

Julian gestured with an open hand. Defeated, Harlan reluctantly reached into his coat pocket and removed the notes.

'You wanted us to fend for ourselves – guess that came back to bite you, didn't it? Things have a way of doing that around you, Julian.'

Julian reached for the money but Harlan moved his hand away.

'Maybe I ought to remind you how being on the other end of this feels,' Julian said, nodding to the ibis.

Harlan swiftly reached inside his coat and grabbed his own ibis, aiming it level with Julian's chest.

The sudden, hostile movements caught the attention of a few commuters.

'Really?' Julian said quietly. 'You're really going to do this here, in front of everyone?'

He turned to a pair of men who were watching them. 'If you thought we were going to have a lightsabre duel, you're mistaken, I'm afraid,' he said with a grin, limply presenting the black baton. 'Just a toy.'

Harlan pushed past Julian, but as he looked up he noticed Elsa at the far end of the station. She was suspiciously hurrying away from a ticket window with her hood up.

'Elsa!' he called out, speeding towards her. 'Elsa, come back!'

By the time Harlan reached her, Elsa had passed through the ticket barriers.

'I'm sorry,' she said shamefully, and lowered her head.

Harlan exhaled. 'You're leaving us? But after everything –'

She had tears in her eyes. 'I can't do this any more!'

'You'll be walking right into their hands,' he said. 'They'll be looking for you. You're making a mistake, Elsa. We already talked about this; we all agreed!'

Elsa shrugged. 'Maybe,' she said. 'Maybe you're right.' *But maybe I am.*

'Don't you want to know *why* you were taken? Or who was behind it?' Harlan's voice grew desperate. 'We have to do this together, just like we said . . .'

'I don't care,' she said. 'I don't care about any of it. I just – I just want to be with my family. Bye, Harlan. *I'm sorry.*'

She turned and sprinted along the platform to the waiting train.

22

A short while after leaving the underpass, Alyn trotted along the side of the road with his thumb outstretched, hoping for some generous stranger to stop. He walked for miles, shivering in the slicing winds stirred by the speeding traffic, before a car pulled over.

'I'm going to London,' he said desperately to the figure inside. 'Any chance of a lift?'

The driver studied him for a couple of seconds, nodded and gestured for him to get in. Resting his head against the rattling window, Alyn watched vacantly as the procession of motorway lights strobed past, blurring into a single neon spool.

After leaving the car near Victoria station, Alyn spent the early hours of the morning navigating a puzzle of deserted, hostile-seeming backstreets and empty roads. Using little more than a mix of signposts, directions from the occasional, abrupt solitary walker and a touch or two of luck, Alyn journeyed deeper into the city and, before long, Pillar presented itself on the horizon, shamelessly dominant.

There it is, he thought, glancing at the torn newspaper article in his hand. *That's where I'll find him.*

It was seven in the morning and still dark when Alyn eventually arrived at the base of the skyscraper. The city was gradually beginning to assemble before his eyes. He looked in the doorway at the electric barriers and at the security guard ambling nearby. Alyn paused, and withdrew.

How am I going to get inside? Alyn thought, looking for some other way. The glass monolith towered over him, icy and solemn, choked by morning fog. He studied the guard, who was shuffling his weight back and forth. The guard waved to a cleaner who was marching up the steps and glanced at his reflection, turning his face to the side.

Alyn crept quietly towards the barriers, willing that the guard's narcissism would be enough to keep him occupied for a few more moments.

Giving him a final look, Alyn ran at the barriers, threw his legs as high as he could, and hit the ground. He rolled on his side and the momentum carried him to his feet. He looked over his shoulder and turned up the collar of his leather jacket.

'JF Industries,' he murmured to himself, pressing the button for the lift. *That's Felix's company.*

Before long, the lift arrived and Alyn selected the twenty-third floor.

When the doors opened, Alyn checked both ways and

hurried round the corridor before eventually finding an office labelled:

CHIEF EXECUTIVE

This must be his office. Alyn tried the door but it was locked.

He continued down the passageway before coming across the boardroom. Some voices from further along the corridor filled him with alarm. Alyn tried the lock, expecting resistance, but it gave. He hurried inside and darted behind the door. The balmy office warmth began to thaw his face, and his nose started to stream.

'Thank you,' came a voice from outside the door, as a shadowy shape stepped into view. 'I'll be seeing you soon.'

Alyn lowered himself and crawled over to a cabinet. He clambered behind it and watched as the door opened and a white-haired man wearing a suit and gold-rimmed glasses entered.

It's Felix, Alyn realized, and his heart began to quicken.

Humming serenely to himself, Felix walked over to the table and straightened a wad of papers.

Alyn looked through the frosted-glass walls and waited until a couple of shapes passed. Then he stood up.

Felix jumped and released the papers on to the floor. 'Who are you? How did you get in here?' he said, jabbing the light switch and pausing as the identity of the boy became clear. 'Alyn.'

'So you *do* remember me,' Alyn said, staring at him. 'You were there, that night. The night I was taken.'

Before Felix had the chance to speak, the door opened and in stepped a security guard. He looked at Felix, then Alyn. 'Sir, we saw an intruder on the camera – are you OK?'

Felix turned to Alyn with a smile. 'Apparently we know each other. Is that right, young man?'

'Yeah. We've met.'

The security guard marched towards Alyn.

'Wait,' Felix ordered, raising his hand. 'Let him finish.'

'It was that night, the night my dad took me to the pub. He was playing cards. We had an argument and I left, remember? It was you who found me later that night. And then you shot me ... with the ibis –' Alyn stopped, realizing Felix was smiling.

'I don't know who you are, but you have quite an imagination.'

'You're a liar!' Alyn yelled and turned to the guard. 'He's a liar, I swear it – he's evil ... he's *evil*!'

The security guard grabbed Alyn and pulled him away from Felix.

'Let go of me!' Alyn snapped, harassed. 'Get your hands off me!'

'Take it easy on him, won't you?' said Felix. 'The boy is obviously disturbed.'

Felix looked at Alyn a final time, adjusted his tie and walked out.

Alyn, struggling with the guard, managed to shout

'*Liar!*' a final time, before being dragged out of the boardroom and into the lift.

After being thrown out of Pillar, Alyn sat on a bench a short way from the skyscraper, with his head planted despondently in his hands.

It was him, Alyn confirmed, as if to reassure himself that he wasn't going mad. *It was him*. And now his only chance of finding an explanation was gone. Hungry and weak, he felt inside his pocket for the coins Anton had given him.

He gathered up the remaining coins and walked across the square to a small coffee shop. The thick, syrupy scent of freshly roasted coffee and toasted bread coiled towards him, luring him closer. Face pressed against the chilled glass, Alyn watched the eager queue inch slowly along. An array of sandwiches and cakes and rolls was displayed temptingly behind a glass counter.

He was about to head inside when he noticed something in the reflection. A telephone box, fifty metres or so away.

'*Dad*,' Alyn said quickly, as soon as the call was answered. 'Dad, it's me . . . It's Alyn.'

There was a moment's pause. 'Who?'

'Me,' Alyn said. 'You know, *your son*. Can you hear me?'

'Yeah, I hear you,' his father slurred. 'We were wondering when you'd turn up.'

'When I'd turn up? What's that supposed to mean? I didn't do this on purpose.'

'So why are you calling?' his father mumbled. 'You obviously want something. Money? Is that it? Money? Always money with you kids –'

'Dad, I didn't run away . . . I was taken . . . kidnapped.'

'You were kidnapped,' his father said. 'By who? Where have you been?'

'In a prison! There were loads of us. We didn't know why we were there . . . they wouldn't say. I mean, they said we were all criminals but we knew we hadn't done anything. And there's this man, Felix . . . a billionaire . . . he's involved –'

'A prison. You were taken to a prison,' his father repeated, stumbling over his words. 'You on drugs, Alyn? I knew it! I knew there was always something funny about you –'

'Dad, you're not listening. *I didn't do anything!* None of us did. We were kidnapped!' Alyn looked at the display. 'I don't have long left. I'm in London. You need to help me. Please, Dad. I need your help.'

'It's not the first time you've run away, is it, Alyn?' his father said. His alcohol-sodden voice turned sharp. 'Your . . . your foster parents told me all about you.'

'No, that was different, I –'

'I mean, I didn't even want to be back in your life, for Christ's sake,' his father snarled. 'It was them who got in touch with me. Them who begged me to try to speak to you.'

'Dad –'

'Why do you think we even gave you up in the first place?'

The telephone went dead.

Alyn felt numb, and trembling he returned the phone to the hook and bit hard into his lip until he felt blood, which he sucked away with his tongue. He turned to the door and pushed it open, but stopped when he saw a paper note stuck to the glass.

COME BACK TONIGHT.
ALONE.
JF

23

After a long night alone, huddled and shivering in a shop doorway, Julian was beginning to question his sense in dismissing Harlan's company so soon. As much as he hated to admit it, he found himself filled with admiration for what he and Elsa had endured since the group's arrival in the city two days ago.

Julian trudged to the newsagent's at the end of the road, past a grubby-looking laundrette and a bookmaker's, and bought himself a sandwich and a bottle of water with the handful of change he had left. He was disposing of the sandwich wrapper when he noticed a charity shop was just opening up on the other side of the road.

He pinched the damp grey uniform beneath his coat with his forefinger and thumb and gazed at the display in the window.

'I'll give you fifty pence for it,' Julian said with a sigh to the bemused-looking lady behind the counter. 'Final offer.'

She snatched the green jumper, glaring at him. 'You have some nerve, trying to haggle in a charity shop . . .'

'You drive a hard bargain.' Julian sighed as his fingers located the last couple of coins. '*Sixty* pence then.'

'*Five pounds*. All money goes to helping disadvantaged children.'

'I *am* a disadvantaged child ... so why don't I just take this,' he said, pulling the jumper back out of her hands, 'and save you the bother of a transaction ...'

The woman grabbed the jumper and tugged, not expecting Julian to maintain his grip. The fabric tore, leaving a frayed wool sleeve dangling in her hand.

'Well, how about that?' Julian pondered, unabashed. 'I'm glad I didn't spend five pounds on it ...'

'Out!' the woman hissed, pointing at the door. 'And don't bother coming back.'

'We can't go it alone,' Julian declared, after finding Harlan sitting in a backstreet near the station a little while later. 'We need to stick together. That money was an easy steal. To tell you the truth, I didn't even take it – I found it on the seat! I'm not cut out for this any more than you are, Harlan.'

Harlan shrugged, sipping his cup of coffee. 'What do you want me to say?'

'Nothing – I want you to listen to my offer. The two of us work together. Now that little brat's gone, it'll be much easier. Three's a crowd, as they say. No dead weight.'

'Whatever happened to fending for yourself? If I remember, that was your motto until Elsa took your money.'

'OK, so maybe it's not as easy as I thought,' Julian admitted begrudgingly. 'But as a matter of fact, Harlan, I've always thought you were the most sensible out of the bunch – which isn't saying much, I know, but still . . .'

Harlan watched him suspiciously.

'You and me try to solve this whole thing,' Julian said, 'together. *Now*.'

Harlan said nothing, enjoying the desperation in Julian's face.

'Goodbye, Julian,' he said, getting to his feet and walking away.

Julian removed the ibis from inside his coat and stormed after him. 'I'm the only one with a chance of surviving this thing and you turn me *down*?'

'You'd sell me out the second it benefits you.' Harlan sighed, not looking back at him. 'Been there, done that.'

Blind with rage, Julian aimed the weapon at Harlan and squeezed the trigger. The blast whizzed by, missing Harlan by centimetres. Harlan turned round and, seeing Julian with his weapon raised, he reached for his own.

Julian fired another blast. Harlan darted on to the next road. He sprinted round some parked cars and ducked behind a white van.

'You've got no idea!' Julian yelled. 'If it weren't for me, you'd all still be back there, rotting in that prison!'

As he approached the van, Harlan sneaked out from behind. He pointed the ibis at Julian's hand and fired. Julian cried out and his arm went instantly limp, flinging his ibis some way along the pavement.

The ibis cracked open and separated into two parts.

Julian exhaled. 'You've broken it!' he said, rushing over and reaching down with his other arm to gather the pieces.

'You were firing at me, idiot!' Harlan panted. 'What did you expect me to do?'

Julian was frantically trying to piece the weapon together.

Harlan knelt down and pulled the pieces towards him. 'It's not broken – see? It just slots back together.'

Wheezing, Julian shot him a thankful look.

'You know, I could finish you off right now, Julian,' Harlan threatened. 'You're lucky there was no one around, or we'd probably be seeing the inside of a cell for real.'

'You know my promises are meaningless,' said Julian. 'But next time I'll think before I shoot. Happy now?'

Harlan muttered something under his breath. He positioned the sections of the ibis together and was about to snap them back into place when he noticed something.

'Look here,' he said, running his finger across the innermost compartment and finding some raised lettering in the plastic. 'A name.'

'The manufacturer,' Julian replied. 'In that case, we might be able to trace it.' He snatched the ibis from Harlan and tilted it towards the sky. 'It looks like it says SIGIL . . .'

Harlan took the ibis back and examined the writing.

'This could be a good lead,' Julian said. 'If SIGIL are supplying weapons to a conspiracy, that must mean they're involved. Now we just need to do some digging on them –'

'*We?* After everything I've said, Julian, you still think I want anything to do with you?'

Julian stared at him blankly.

'There's something I've been waiting for from you,' Harlan said. 'And, before I consider agreeing, I'm going to need it.'

Julian remained blank. 'You know I don't have any money left . . .'

Harlan shook his head.

'And you're not taking my ibis,' Julian said, pulling it to his chest defensively.

'I don't want your ibis; I have my own. I want an apology.'

'Oh.' Julian considered this for a moment. 'Then I'm sorry, I suppose. Now can we get on with finding them?'

24

Elsa left the train and sprinted as quickly as she could along the platform.

The journey felt like it had taken forever: a lot of sneaking, hopping ticket barriers and hiding. She'd got lost a few times trying to navigate an array of trains, and at one point she thought she'd almost ended up on her way back to Scotland and had to spend the night at a station because she'd missed the last train. Biting back tears of frustration, she was helped the following morning by a concerned elderly man who thought she might be lost and offered to take her to the nearest police station. Still suspicious of any authority, Elsa politely declined and left.

Eventually, she found her train. Too excited to sleep, her eyes followed the sliding landscape, eager to see some – *any* – indication that she was moving closer to home.

Despite what Harlan probably thought, she hadn't planned to make such a sudden exit. Perhaps, if they'd found the others, she might have stayed. But with just the two of them, barely enough money to last more than a few more days, and the increasing suspicion that they were being stalked, Elsa felt she had little choice.

Her only regret was not having the chance to say goodbye – *a proper goodbye*.

Once out of the station, she ran, wind tearing at her, the pavement bouncing, dancing madly. She sprinted across the road, not even waiting for the traffic lights, through the park, across the grass, ignoring the barking dogs.

Elsa leant down, coughing, her chest and lungs on fire. Up ahead, at the end of the road, she could see her house.

I made it! I really made it. And no sign of any kidnappers anywhere.

Satisfied that she had proven Harlan and the others wrong, Elsa rose up straight and started to jog on, imagining how her mother and father and brother, Simon, might react, and what she might say to them. Chances were they would think she had gone mad, but she was sure she could convince them. Eventually, anyway.

She paused at the traffic lights, giddy with excitement, when a car screeched to a halt in front of her.

'Hey!' Elsa cried, hopping back. 'You almost ran me over!'

Before she could take another step a hand reached out of the door, took her arm and pulled her in.

25

Jes was sitting cross-legged on the floor while Henry searched a bag in the corner of the room. He eventually removed a candle.

'Maybe we should wait for Ryan,' said Henry.

'I wouldn't waste your time,' Jes answered. 'He doesn't believe it.'

'He will.' With this, Henry lifted the candle up and sparked his lighter, waiting for the flame to take. 'What about you?'

'I don't know yet,' Jes said, watching the swaying flame. 'But I *want* to believe it. Who wouldn't?'

Henry set the candle down in front of her. Ryan crept up to the door and crooked his neck to watch. Jes took a deep breath and sat in silence for a few minutes. She opened her eyes.

'Nothing's happening,' she said, sighing. 'I can't put out the flame.'

'If you're having trouble keeping your concentration, you can use a locus.'

'What's that?'

'It could be anything – an object, or even a word, a sound ... a picture. It's usually best if you choose something meaningful.'

Jes closed her eyes again, and began repeating a word under her breath. Ryan leant in a little closer, hoping it might be his name she was repeating. Unfortunately it sounded like *Alyn*.

'I need to make a phone call,' Henry said, and moved towards the door. 'Keep practising.'

Ryan pulled away and ducked round the corner, hiding in a shadowy corridor. He could see Henry walk to the end of the tunnel and stand beside the ladder. Ryan watched as he removed his phone from his pocket. 'Charlie,' Henry said, lowering his voice. 'Are you on your way?'

Ryan leant forward, straining his ears.

'They're to be taken back to the headquarters in the city,' Henry continued. 'Ryan is showing some promise, but Jes's Ability is very weak. They've both got a long way to go. They're not going to like it, but do *not* let them leave. No matter what they tell you.'

Do not let them leave? Ryan dashed back into the room where Jes was practising.

She gasped. 'Ryan! You made me jump.'

'Hey,' Ryan whispered. 'I just heard Henry talking outside. This Guild's not what we think.'

'What?'

'They don't trust us by ourselves. They're gonna take us to their headquarters and keep us there.'

'They think we'll end up getting ourselves caught?' Jes said, as though confirming what he had heard.

'Yep. I heard him say under no circumstances to let us go. That isn't what we signed up for. I mean, what about the others? What about the Pledge? We can't just sit back.'

The sound of Henry's footsteps made Ryan lower his voice. 'I'm sick of being a prisoner!' he exclaimed. 'I say we go ourselves, and forget about this whole Guild thing. What do you say?'

26

'Sit,' Stephen said, as Susannah cautiously opened the door to his office. A giant portrait of him grinned at her from the wall, and seemed to follow her as she walked over to his desk.

'I'm sorry I'm late, Mr Nover,' she said. 'The helicopter couldn't take off until the snowstorm settled.'

Ignoring her, Stephen swivelled his chair to the side. 'It seems like you've had quite a time up there with all the action.'

Stephen reached into his desk drawer and removed a snarling fox mask. He held it over his face, watching Susannah. 'It's for the masquerade ball,' he explained. 'Some stupid charity affair later this week.'

'It's realistic,' she said, looking a little uncomfortable. 'Very realistic.'

'Because it's real, that's why!' He giggled and tossed the mask across to her. It landed face up in her lap. 'Daddy got it for me while he was hunting. I made the taxidermist make it look as fierce as he could.'

Susannah ran an uncomfortable finger along the fur.

Stephen leant back in his chair. 'What? You don't like it?'

'I quite like foxes,' Susannah replied.

'Oh. Well, in that case, put it on.'

'I'd – I'd rather not, if you don't mind.' She picked up the mask between her forefinger and thumb and placed it on his desk.

Stephen smirked playfully. 'I'm not going to tell you again, Ms Dion.' He picked up the mask and presented it to her. '*Put it on.*'

Susannah reached out reluctantly to take the mask. As her fingers neared, he let out a loud bark.

Susannah jumped and Stephen threw his head back, giggling. 'The look on your face,' he said. 'A picture!'

'Has there been any progress with finding the inmates?' Susannah asked, keen to change the subject, as Stephen placed the mask on the desk again facing her.

'Not yet. But our men are closing in.' Stephen smiled. 'It won't be long now before they have something, or someone, to show.'

Susannah exhaled. 'Thank God.'

'Hm. Yes, anyway, I just wanted to check up on something – our arrangement regarding Felix's company.'

'What about it?'

'I want you to increase the subliminal messages. I want ten frames per lesson, showing the value of his company decreasing.'

Susannah pondered. 'Ten frames is a lot,' she said.

'I don't think you understand, but using the Ability that much to manipulate reality has consequences for the children . . .'

'Oh, I understand perfectly well,' Stephen said. His eyes were unblinking. 'It gives them headaches. It exhausts them. It makes them weak. Nonsense! The little rascals have never done a day's work in their lives, unlike some of us. Increase the frequency, Ms Dion. Do it immediately. At once. I need to overtake Felix as soon as possible!'

Susannah sighed. 'I'm just not sure it's a good idea . . .'

Stephen held up the fox mask in front of his face. 'Do it, Ms Dion,' he said in a pantomime snarl. 'Do it or I'll come and eat you while you sleep!'

'How long?' she asked wearily.

'A week!' Stephen said. 'Now go to the roof. The helicopter will be waiting to take you back to the prison.'

'Yes, sir.' Susannah stood. 'What about my bonus, Mr Nover?' she added hesitantly.

'Make sure Felix's fortune suffers, and you'll get your bonus. Cheerio.'

Susannah nodded and hurried quickly out of the room.

Stephen squealed with delight and picked up the mask, poking his fingers through the eyeholes like writhing worms.

27

'SIGIL is a British technology company, dealing with cutting-edge research,' Harlan read from the computer screen in the empty Internet cafe. 'It is one of the numerous companies owned by Stephen Nover –'

'Oh, anyone but him,' Julian muttered, folding his arms.

Harlan looked at Julian. 'You know him?'

Know him? Julian thought. *You can barely open a newspaper without seeing his smug face.* 'The media fawns over him,' he spat. 'They never seem to tire of telling us how wonderful he is. He's even got this army of militant fans. They call themselves "Nover-dosers".' Julian rolled his eyes.

Harlan returned to the screen. 'You sound jealous.'

Julian glared at him. 'I'm not jealous, Harlan. But I'm not surprised either. He's the sort of person who would sell out his own grandmother, given the chance.'

'I don't know how you aren't choking on your words,' Harlan said, looking sideways at his companion.

'Oh, just get on with it,' Julian said, nodding towards the computer.

Harlan clicked on Stephen's name and followed the link to a biography page.

'Stephen Nover is an English business magnate, entrepreneur, television personality, ambassador and philanthropist . . .'

On the right-hand side was a photograph of a smiling Stephen, standing with a grateful crowd of children outside a hospital. A cartoonishly oversized cheque was poised generously in his hands.

Harlan shrugged. 'Seems like a nice guy. Just look at the list of stuff he's done for charity over the years. You think we might have the wrong guy, or –'

'Or he's got something to hide. Stephen's company's name is on the ibis. I've never seen or heard about an ibis outside the prison. As far as I'm concerned, that makes him guilty.' *And puts us one step ahead.*

Feeling a little self-satisfied, Julian leant back in his chair, clasping his hands behind his head.

'Remember why we're going after him, though, Julian,' Harlan said. 'I don't want you turning this into some personal thing because you don't like the guy.'

'Promise,' Julian said, crossing his fingers behind his head.

'And whether or not he's involved, we've still got a problem,' said Harlan. 'And that's how we track down the second-richest man in the country.'

'We don't track him down,' Julian said, pushing away from the desk. 'We draw him *out*. And I know how.'

28

'Just let me go,' Elsa begged, trying to free herself. 'Please . . . my house is just there . . . it's just there!'

The young woman in the passenger seat looked at the man next to her, then turned her eyes back to the road. She picked up a list – Elsa could make out the word 'Inmates' at the top – and thumbed through a couple of pages. 'Who else escaped with you?'

'I'm not saying anything,' Elsa sobbed. 'You can't make me say anything!' She pressed her face against the window. *If only I'd stayed with Harlan, this would never have happened.* 'You can't make me go back to the prison. You can't –'

The woman cut her off with a stare. 'We're not taking you back to the prison.'

Elsa caught her breath and looked up. 'You mean you're not *them*?'

'We're not *them*. We're people like you. I'm Pyra. This is Anton.'

Elsa's head throbbed. She wiped her face against the

seat. 'So where are you taking me? Why did you just drag me into the car? Couldn't you . . . just have asked?'

'In our experience that doesn't tend to work,' Anton said.

'Why aren't you telling me anything! Who are you?'

'There's a way we do things,' he went on. 'There are going to be things that we tell you that will turn your sense of reality completely on its head. You'll need to be prepared and we don't want to overload you with information.' He tapped his head.

Elsa leant between the seats. 'You want to know something? My sense of reality is *already* upside down. It has been ever since they put me in that stupid place.'

'Which is why we need to take you now, to protect you,' Pyra said. 'And the others, as many of them as possible.'

Elsa considered this for a moment, and then spoke. 'There's Harlan, he's been looking after me. And Julian. You'll hate Julian at first; he has that effect on people, but he's OK really. Jes and Ryan are still in the forest; I don't know if they're alive. And there's Alyn; no one knows what happened to him either.'

'Alyn's fine,' Pyra said.

'You mean you've seen him? Where? When?'

'We were taking him back to our base but he escaped. We don't know where he is now.'

Elsa exhaled loudly and flopped back in her car seat.

'There's somewhere we can go for now,' said Pyra. 'Somewhere safe.'

'Hang on, does that mean we're *not* safe at the moment?'

Anton caught her eyes in the mirror. 'No. You're not. And that's why we need to find your friends as soon as possible. Because the people we're trying to keep you safe from are already here. They're already looking for you.'

29

Alyn waited until it was dark and walked back to where he could see Pillar rising high above the other skyscrapers.

If Felix even bothers to turn up, who's to say I'm not going to get another barrage of lies? he wondered, torn between whether or not he should comply with the billionaire's request.

He eventually sat on a bench overlooking the river, half expecting to see a gang of armed men approaching him from the shadows at any moment. Several times Alyn considered forgetting about the meeting and running away as far as he could. But then he'd never know. *If Felix wanted me back in the prison, he'd have taken me already*, he thought, unfolding the note.

Garlands of air flowed from his mouth. He fumbled with stiff fingers for the jacket zip and pulled it up to his throat.

'Reminds me of the night we met,' said a voice behind him.

Felix smiled and shuffled on to the bench beside him.

He pushed his gold-rimmed glasses further up his nose and loosened the scarf beneath his overcoat.

You'd better say something, Alyn seethed inwardly, glaring at him.

'I'm sorry, Alyn,' Felix said eventually.

Alyn stood. 'You're sorry . . . you think that's enough? You think that even means anything? After everything you've put us through? You think you can just say you're *sorry*?'

Felix put a hand on the bench and followed Alyn to his feet. 'I'm sure you have a lot of questions.'

'Starting with why you took us and put us in that . . . place. Why did you do it? Why me? Why *us*?'

'We took you against your will,' Felix said. 'We lied, yes. We deceived you. But there was no other way. We had to get you all together. We had to *break* you . . .'

'*Why*?'

Felix took a deep breath. He passed a hand lightly across his white hair. 'I started my own business in my thirties. Things didn't really work out that well to begin with. I suppose I was moderately successful, but –' he removed his glasses and fiddled with the handles – 'but I wanted *more*. Call it ambition, greed, I don't know. Through some fortuitous circumstances I was put in touch with a pair of researchers. Psychologists. They were studying *luck*, or rather the luckiest people they could find.'

'I don't see where this is going,' Alyn said impatiently.

Felix ignored him. 'As they continued studying these people, these almost supernaturally lucky people, they discovered something: that these people were able to change things. *Reality*. A lot of the time they had no idea they were even doing it.'

'They could change reality,' Alyn repeated. 'You really just said that?'

'Yes.'

'Like a superpower?'

Felix considered this for a moment. 'Not really. Something a little more subtle. I understand your scepticism, Alyn. I was sceptical myself – as anyone would be.'

Felix rubbed his brow. 'I was the only person in the world to know about this Ability, other than the pair who had discovered it. After some negotiation, we struck up a deal and I ... I employed five of these gifted individuals to work for my company. We set up a very basic – perhaps a little crude – method of getting them to unconsciously alter reality. To nudge things in my favour, without them knowing.'

'That's how you became so rich,' said Alyn quietly.

Felix nodded. 'The strategy has its limits. It does not make miracles or subvert the laws of physics. It nudges chance to fall in our favour; it beckons fate with a playful finger.'

'And that's what you've been doing?' Alyn said, raking his fingers through his hair. 'You've been using us. Manipulating us. You spliced images in the videos ... so people didn't consciously see them. To make *you* richer!'

'Not to make me richer –' he gestured around him – 'for

the sake of everything. For the greater good. We've seen the results. *It works*, Alyn. It really works! We're changing the world. *You* are changing the world and if it weren't for you, the country would be in ruin already. This time last year, one of our largest banks was on the verge of collapse, which would've devastated our already fragile economy. Using your Ability, which we'd harnessed, we were able to influence some key players to keep their money invested. That bank has now almost recovered. We've had assassination attempts on politicians thwarted – bullets that have missed, bombs that have failed to detonate. A war almost broke out in one of our overseas territories until we used you all to influence peace. What could have been a massacre ended after forty-five minutes with barely a casualty. The unrest is beginning to subside. Things are getting better, Alyn. They aren't there yet, but two years – that's all it will take – and we'll enter a new era ... an era of peace and prosperity, and it'll all be down to you, and the other children who are still there.'

He really believes it, Alyn thought, backing away. *He sounds like some crazy cult leader ...*

'Why did you have to put us through all of this – *kidnapping us* – lying to us?' Alyn's voice began to rise.

'It was for the greater good!' Felix said, justifying himself.

'There are nearly a hundred kids trapped in that place, scared to death, believing every word of it! What about them? What about their parents? You've caused so much suffering –'

'What other way could there have been, Alyn? We knock at the door and *ask* your parents for their permission to take you? This had to be done in secret. The lies were all necessary to keep you in place. And, for the most part, it seemed to work . . . You and the rest of those children have saved hundreds of thousands of lives.'

Alyn stared vacantly at the glowing buildings around them.

'There is another group, the *Guild* as they call themselves, operating in the shadows with a far darker aim. The Pledge is trying to bring about order and harmony . . . to make the country, the world, a better place. But the Guild has been trying to attack and hinder us at every turn. And that's why we need you on our side, Alyn. That's why we need all of you.'

'Why are you here . . . ? Why are you telling me this?'

'That night I took you, I saw your father – the way he treated you. I felt desperately sorry for you. My ex-wife and I, we were never able to have children. I have no heir, no inheritor. What I want is an apprentice. And one with your gifts would be extremely encouraging.'

Felix pointed to a nearby skyscraper, overlooking the Thames. 'Do you see that penthouse, Alyn? Right at the top there?'

Alyn shielded his eyes and nodded.

'Say yes, Alyn, and it is yours. The apartment, an excellent wage, prestige. You'll never need nor want for anything ever again. Say yes and all of it is yours.'

30

Ryan beckoned for Jes to slip out of the door after him.

Shivering, the pair tiptoed down the corridor, shifting on to the balls of their feet round the puddles.

Jes manoeuvred past one of the larger patches of water and gripped the ladder. The lid was already half-off.

We'd better be quick. He probably wasn't planning on being gone long, Ryan thought.

He followed her and waited as she began to climb. At the top, Jes pulled herself on to the snow and lay holding her side.

He appeared a few moments later and crawled towards her. 'You OK?' he asked.

Jes nodded and rose up slowly.

Ryan leant down and dragged the lid across the hole. *Good riddance to him and his stupid magic tricks*, he thought.

When he turned back round, Jes was reaching into the snow. She removed a large jagged rock the size of a tennis ball and brushed away the snow with her fingertips.

'What's that for?'

'In case we get into any trouble,' Jes answered coolly.

Ryan felt a little uncomfortable at hearing this. He said nothing and headed through the trees. Snow was swirling in front of him as the wind picked up. Behind him, Jes's footsteps crunched and squeaked in the snow.

'You know the way, Ryan?' she called across to him.

'This is the only way I haven't been yet.'

He removed the ibis from his pocket. *They were exposed here, vulnerable, and a run-in with the guards wouldn't end well. Maybe Henry had a point.*

They walked together for another hundred or so metres when Ryan spotted a familiar black uniform.

Ryan lifted the ibis in both hands and closed one eye. He was about to squeeze the trigger when he spotted a second guard, and then a third.

'We should probably run,' Jes said behind him, lowering the rock.

She grabbed Ryan's arm and turned, to find a guard standing directly behind them. The man raised his ibis, but Ryan fired first. The man flew back into a tree.

'There they are!' shouted one of the men in the distance.

We're trapped, Ryan thought. *We'll never get away.*

'This way,' Jes said, trying her best to run. Her hand fell to her side and she let out a cry.

'Get behind the tree,' Ryan hissed. He dropped to his knees, steadying his hand, and fired. The shot missed.

One of the guards fired his own weapon, and Ryan only just moved out of the way in time.

He scrambled to his feet and raced towards where Jes was hiding. 'There are too many of them,' he panted. He passed the ibis to Jes. 'I'll try to hold 'em off. You head back to the tunnel, get Henry.'

'There's no need,' said a disappointed-looking Henry, who appeared behind them. '*This* is why I told you both to stay put.'

'Look, we're sorry,' Ryan said, anxiously peering out from the tree.

Henry ignored him and pointed through the trees. 'Go two miles east and you'll see a car arriving soon. It'll be one of my people.'

'We're not leaving you here,' Jes said. 'This is our fault! We'll stay and fight –'

'With what, that rock?' Henry said. 'We're outnumbered. You need to get as far away from here as possible.'

'But what about the –'

'I've dealt with worse,' Henry said, and tried to smile.

'Come on,' Ryan said, pulling Jes towards him. He looked at Henry, offering him a brief nod in parting.

The pair darted through the trees, not looking back, flinching only at the sound of a solitary ibis blast, and the sound of something heavy falling quietly into the powdery snow.

31

'We're here,' Pyra said, opening the car door.

'So is this your headquarters?' Elsa hopped out, tilting her neck back at the neglected block of flats in front of her. *Looks like somewhere you wouldn't want to hang around alone*, she thought, gazing at the mass of criss-crossed wires and the grubby satellite dishes, some of which seemed slumped with shame. A gang of teenage boys sat sullenly on bikes in a deserted playground not far from the flats. Behind her was a busy main road and a few faceless offices scattered behind it.

'Are you coming, or what?' Pyra said by the door.

Elsa nodded, running towards her. *Hermes House*, she read, looking at the peeling sign above.

Pyra jabbed a code on a grey metal box on the wall. There was a buzz, and the gated door creaked open.

'Ugh, what's that smell?' Elsa said, pulling a face. Bits of litter floated around aimlessly in the breezy hallway. She scurried after Pyra and Anton to the tiny lift in the centre of a winding stairwell. Some graffiti had been scrawled on one of the metal panels and the floor was covered in muddy footprints.

'This lift is safe, right?' Elsa said, gripping the handrail as it began to rise.

Anton shrugged. 'I've only been stuck in it once or twice.'

Elsa's eyes widened.

'Just kidding,' he said with a grin.

The lift soon came to an excruciatingly slow halt. Elsa breathed a sigh of relief as the doors peeled open, and paused. She was on the top floor of what seemed, at first glance, to be a palace.

Large stone columns rose up from the tiled stone floor with its enormous eight-pointed star, which Elsa followed with her eyes to a row of windows, giving a sweeping view over the streets and houses below. Above her was a cream-coloured coffered ceiling, while to the far side of the room was an ominous set of oak doors, guarded by two statues on either side.

'Whoa,' Elsa said. She walked round one of the columns to a large circular table, covered in scraps of paper and photographs. 'This is the coolest thing ever. How do you keep something like this hidden?'

Pyra walked over to the window. 'You saw what it looked like from the outside. No one would ever think of looking.'

Elsa peered out of the window on tiptoes. 'So they're fake satellite dishes and everything! Ha! So this whole building is yours?'

'Yep. It's ours,' Pyra said.

As Elsa was about to embark on a second survey of the room, a bald man in his early forties appeared. His face was covered in deep-set wrinkles and he wore a black long-sleeved shirt. 'You must be Elsa,' he said. 'You were one of the prisoners.'

'Yeah,' Elsa said, still gazing around. 'How do you know my name?'

'My name is Luthan. I'm in charge while our leader, Henry, is otherwise engaged,' he said, ignoring her question.

'So what do you guys *do* here?'

'We find people like you,' Luthan said. 'We train them.'

'Train them to do what?'

Luthan smiled. 'To use the gift that you, and all the others, possess. We call it the Ability.'

'Cool! So when are you going to train me?'

'That depends on whether or not you're ready,' Luthan answered. 'But right now you must be tired, Elsa,' he continued. 'I'll show you to your room.'

'My room? Hang on, you mean I'm staying here?'

'People are looking for you and the rest of your friends. You really think they would risk you all running free? They aren't going to stop until they find each of you. And if Pyra and Anton managed to find you that easily . . . those people won't be far behind.'

I need to find the others, Elsa thought, suddenly worried. 'Can I go home?'

Luthan shook his head. 'It's not safe for you to go home. We have to keep you here to protect you.'

'So you're the good guys then?'

'"Good" is a funny word, Elsa,' said Luthan. 'Your room is this way.' He beckoned for her to follow him.

Elsa went after him through the oak doors to an adjoining corridor. A couple of men and a woman with short blonde hair quickly ended their conversation and watched them walk by.

'They don't seem very friendly,' Elsa whispered, tugging Luthan's sleeve.

'You've all been kidnapped and held as prisoners. They're probably not sure what to say.'

Elsa looked back over her shoulder at the group.

'Don't worry,' Luthan said. 'I'll make sure you're all properly introduced later.'

'So how many of you are here?' Elsa said.

'There are twelve of us. Hopefully more, if we can find your friends. Now, your room is just here . . .'

Elsa started to push open the nearest door, but found it locked.

'Not in there,' Luthan quickly said. 'Come away from there, please.'

Drawn to the door, Elsa stopped and studied it for a few moments. 'What's in here?'

Luthan gently guided her away. 'You're allowed in any room here except that one, Elsa.'

'Structural damage,' Pyra said from behind. 'You wouldn't want the ceiling falling on you, would you?'

Elsa shook her head vigorously from side to side.

Luthan walked over to another room and held the door open for her. 'In you go,' he said.

Elsa slipped inside. Apart from two beds and a desk in the corner, the room was bare. There was a pile of folded clothes on one of the beds.

She exhaled. 'A bed. You've no idea how pleased I am to see one of these!'

Elsa ran to the bed and threw herself at it with such force she almost bounced straight back off. She extended her arms, affixing herself tightly to the mattress.

'Before you rest, I do have a few questions, Elsa. While you were in the prison, did you find out anything at all about the people who were in charge?'

'Like what?' asked Elsa.

'Any names?'

'Yeah, we found out one man's name,' Elsa said. 'Felix. I don't know who that is, but we know he has something to do with it. Something important, I'd say.'

Luthan raised his eyes to the window. 'James Felix. Just as we thought.'

'You know him?'

'He's the richest man in the country,' Luthan answered distantly. 'Are you quite sure this is what you heard?'

'Yeah, it was just after we escaped! We stole the teacher's phone and found his name in it. We even called him and everything.' With this, Elsa gave out a loud yawn.

'That'll be enough for now. Thank you, Elsa. Dinner will be at six,' Luthan said. 'You're free to rest until then.'

Elsa's stomach ached at the thought of food. 'I'll be there,' she murmured contentedly. Then with a great deal of effort, she pulled herself off the bed. 'Hey, can I ask something?'

'Of course. You can ask me anything.'

'The catch. I mean, there must be a catch, right? You letting me stay here and all.'

Luthan shook his head. 'No catch. Your friends will stay here too.'

'Yeah, about that – I left Harlan back at the station. Who knows where he is now. And Julian's floating around too.'

'We'll get looking for them straight away,' Pyra added, peering round the door.

'We need to free all the other kids back at the prison too, right?' Elsa said, tiredness building in her voice. 'We need to show them they can't just go kidnapping us for no reason!'

'Our leader, Henry, is already there. He's been figuring out the next step. We can't just *crash* in unannounced.'

Elsa gave a murmur of approval before sinking into the mattress. She was buzzing with enough excitement that she stayed awake for a further five minutes, but not a second longer.

32

Harlan held the small printed map steady between both hands as it flapped in the window. 'Nover has three offices scattered around London. Two are over here.' He circled an area with his finger.

Julian seemed sceptical. 'And then what? We approach the second-wealthiest man in the country, just like *that*?' Julian snapped his fingers to illustrate the apparently absurd ease of Harlan's plan.

'We find a way to sneak in.' Harlan folded the map and put it back inside his pocket. 'Maybe we could find some uniforms or something. Disguise ourselves. There's no way they'd let us in like this. We wait until he's alone and find out exactly who purchased this technology from him.'

'A death trap, in other words,' Julian offered. *And for all we know, he is part of this, not just his weapons.*

'You have a better idea?'

'All of my ideas are better than yours,' Julian quipped. 'No offence.'

'None taken.'

Julian scratched his chin, gazing skywards. 'What we need to do is to let him know we're on to him – a mind like his simply won't resist a game of cat and mouse. We need to draw *him* out.' Julian made sure nobody was watching and removed the ibis. 'This is advanced technology. Cutting-edge, closely guarded. If the ibis technology were made public, it would be quickly replicated.'

'You mean we leak it to the press.' Harlan folded his arms. 'What if he doesn't take the bait?'

'And risk us leaking it? He must've invested hundreds of millions on research. It would be worthless. And, let's not forget, the country's golden boy investing in weapon technology would be sure to raise a few eyebrows.' Julian smiled. 'No. He'll take the bait all right.' He nodded to a telephone box at the end of the road. 'Now do you want to do it, or shall I?'

After quickly deciding who should make the call, Julian headed over, clearing his throat, and running through his opening line in his head.

'I need to speak with Mr Nover immediately,' Julian said as soon as the telephone was answered.

'You would need to speak with his personal secretary,' the receptionist replied, 'and her details are not given out to just anyone. You need an appointment to speak with her.'

'And presumably *her* secretary, and so on, and so on. Utter drivel! In that case I want you to pass on a message to her for me. *Ibis*. I – B – I – S. I'll say that once more.

Eye-bis,' he said, pronouncing each syllable. 'Mr Nover will understand the significance.'

'Whoever you are, I'm sorry,' said the receptionist, 'but I'm not passing on coded messages. This isn't the school playground –'

'This is no coded message,' Julian intervened. 'I have important information regarding the advanced sonic technology that Mr Nover's company SIGIL has developed in secret. If you don't pass on this message, I suggest you start looking for another job, because yours will be gone as soon as Mr Nover realizes your error.'

Julian turned to Harlan with a smug look, then returned his attention to the phone.

After a moment assimilating Julian's threat, the receptionist spoke. 'Who are you?'

'A concerned party. I'm sure Mr Nover can read between the lines, even if you can't. Tell him to call me back on this number as soon as he gets the message.'

Julian read out the telephone-box number and slammed the phone down.

'Convincing,' said an impressed Harlan. 'Now I guess we wait.'

33

'We should've stayed put,' Jes grumbled as they continued as quickly as they could through the forest. 'They'll take Henry back to the prison and they'll torture him until he speaks. I swear if they hurt him, I'll –'

'Calm down,' Ryan said. 'There's nothing the two of us can do anyway, is there?'

Jes said nothing.

'Henry said to go two miles this way,' Ryan went on. 'It shouldn't take too long.'

Jes leant against a tree momentarily, holding her scar.

'Wanna stop?' Ryan asked.

She shook her head. 'We'd better keep going.'

The pair trudged on. Ryan struggled to think of things to say, but gave up after his questions met with little response. His head was soon aching from having to squint so much at the glaring light upon the snow, and his coat was chafing his neck from looking back to make sure Jes was still following.

No wonder they chose to put us here, Ryan thought. Had they not had directions to follow, he may well have given up completely. And who was to say they were walking east? Or that the old man's directions were even right in the first place?

'Look,' Jes said, nodding to a shape between the trees. 'A car.'

Ryan looked up. He gestured for her to halt and lifted the ibis. 'Just being cautious. You go round the back, I'll go the other way.'

They scurried towards the vehicle, each taking a different direction.

'Hey,' Ryan said, pointing his ibis at the shape in the driver's seat. 'Open up.'

The car door opened and out stepped a slim Asian man wearing a baseball cap. He raised his hands in submission.

'Who are you?' Ryan asked, squinting down the weapon.

The man opened his mouth to speak, but paused, taken aback at the pair of them.

'Get talking,' said Jes.

'I'm with the Guild,' the man said.

Ryan and Jes shared a look. Ryan lowered the ibis.

'My name's Charlie,' the man went on. 'Where's Henry? I thought he was supposed to be with you.'

'The guards got him.'

'The guards. You sure about that?'

Ryan nodded and walked round the car, looking in through the window.

'He'll be at the prison now,' said Jes.

Charlie rested a hand wearily on the brim of his cap. 'Get in the car,' he said.

'Think he's mad at us?' Ryan whispered to Jes.

Charlie opened the driver's door and sank on to the seat.

'So what's happening?' asked Ryan when they'd climbed in. 'Are we gonna go and rescue him?'

Charlie shook his head. 'I'm taking you back to our base in London.'

'What about Henry? We can't just leave him there . . .' said Ryan.

'You really think the three of us have a chance? It'd be suicide. You're coming back with me, so you can be with the others. Then we'll figure out what to do.'

'Hold on, what others?' Jes asked. 'You mean they're with you?'

'Well, we're working on it,' Charlie said. He shot them a look in the rear-view mirror and turned on the ignition.

34

'... and then I had to crawl through a vent! I never thought I'd be able to, but we didn't have much choice because I was the only one who fit inside.'

Elsa looked at the surrounding faces in the dining room of the Guild's headquarters. Each of them was watching her, enthralled as she regaled them with the details of the prison escape. The candles on the large rectangular table trembled gently.

'But it all went wrong when Adler took Ryan and put him in solitary. He tried taking me down there too, but I managed to shove him inside and lock the door. And then I –'

'You're thirteen and you managed to escape a prison?' said a man with glasses, clearly impressed.

'*And* they escaped the forest ... and spent a few days sleeping rough on the street,' said another.

Elsa blushed and gave an awkward smile. *This is awesome. They're hanging on my every word*, she thought. 'Well, when you say it like that. Anyway, are you guys still looking for my friends? We need to find them.'

'No sign of them so far. But Pyra and Anton will be leaving first thing tomorrow,' Luthan said. As acting leader, he was seated at the head of the table.

'Great! I'll go with them.'

Luthan smiled sympathetically. 'It'll be safer if you stay here, Elsa. Pyra and Anton are trained.'

'That's not fair!' she pleaded. 'I told you everything about what I did – what *we* did, right?'

'All the more reason for you to stay. You wouldn't want to go back there, would you?'

'Good luck bringing them back without me,' she huffed.

She hopped down from her chair and hurried out of the dining room. In the gymnasium at the end of the corridor, she heard a steady thumping noise. She peered in and saw Anton, throwing a series of kicks at a punch bag hanging from the wall. Sensing her, Anton stopped and looked over his shoulder.

'So you guys are going after Harlan and Julian?' she asked, dropping on to the weightlifting bench.

Anton nodded. He picked up a water bottle and dribbled the contents over his brow.

'I want to come but Luthan won't let me,' Elsa complained. 'But there's no way they'll trust you. You need me there.'

Anton leant down and put the water bottle on the floor. 'All right,' he said, nodding, remembering how Alyn's own lack of trust had caused him to flee. 'I'll have a word with Luthan.'

35

'Feel free to stay here as long as you want while you make up your mind,' Felix said the following morning, gesturing for Alyn to step into the lift of his apartment building. 'It's the least I could do.'

Alyn had spent the past twelve hours in a bus shelter, struggling to make sense of everything Felix had told him. Tired and hungry, he found himself guided by some unseen hand to the billionaire's apartment the next morning, where he was promptly greeted in the lobby by his enthusiastic host.

'You can go in – it's not locked,' Felix said, smiling as the lift doors opened, and he pointed to his apartment.

Alyn looked at him, then entered. The first thing to catch his eye was an enormous crystal chandelier, suspended threateningly above a set of leather sofas. Alyn hesitantly stepped from the floorboards on to a cream rug as he followed Felix to the master bedroom. On a table by the bedroom door was a crystal vase. Alyn's attention was drawn to it immediately.

You've wanted your revenge, he thought, staring at

the back of Felix's head and letting his fingers wrap round the neck of the vase. *Now's your chance . . .*

'Through here is a walk-in wardrobe,' Felix said, gesturing with his hand to an inconspicuous-looking wooden panel.

Alyn released his fingers from the vase as Felix pulled the panel to one side, revealing a narrow room, which extended a considerable way back. Either side was filled with shoeboxes and rows of expensive clothes.

'We're about the same height, aren't we?' Felix said, sizing up his guest. 'Everything in here can be yours. I haven't worn half of it!'

Alyn walked through the room, not saying a word. At the far end was a full-length mirror, throwing back his overwhelmed doppelgänger.

'And over here,' Felix said, leaving the wardrobe, 'is the bathroom. Why don't you take a look inside?'

Felix pointed to a door on the other side of the bedroom. Alyn entered and paused. A circular Jacuzzi gurgled and hummed serenely, surrounded by a ring of flickering candles. In the far corner behind the Jacuzzi was a glass shower area, stocked with bundles of fresh white towels.

'You haven't said much, Alyn,' Felix said. 'Do you like it?'

'Well, yeah,' Alyn said quietly. 'It's amazing.' *It's better than amazing. I've never seen anywhere like this.*

'I'm sure you want some time to think about what I've said.'

'I still haven't forgiven you,' Alyn blurted out, before Felix had the chance to leave.

The ageing billionaire looked at him, mustering a sad smile. 'Come,' he said.

Alyn followed him out of the bathroom and into the kitchen. Felix switched on a television mounted on the wall, which was showing a news broadcast.

'Despite our best efforts, there is still a lot of unrest. Chaos. People feel as though they have nothing left to lose.'

He pointed at the screen. The news broadcast showed a pedestrian street in the centre of London blocked off by the police.

'This happened just last week, Alyn. A gang of terrorists left a chilling threat that they were going to bomb the city.'

'What happened?'

'They didn't,' Felix said. 'We put some subliminal images in the film, so you would all unconsciously influence the bomb to malfunction. Individually, you might only ever influence small things to happen . . . the fall of a coin, but together –'

'We can make miracles happen,' Alyn said aloud. *I remember seeing the images in the film, back at the prison. I didn't think anything of it . . . What else have we been influencing?*

'All those lives,' Felix said, as though reading Alyn's thoughts. 'You're heroes. And you don't even know it.'

Alyn looked away, not quite knowing what to think.

'If you hadn't taken us and kidnapped us, those people would've died . . . ?' he asked.

'That is just one example,' Felix went on. 'If you'd like another, I'd be more than happy to show you.'

'Wait,' Alyn ordered.

'Yes?'

'Back in the prison, there was a girl. Jes. I think something happened to her. I need you to find out for me.'

After a moment's pause, Felix spoke. 'I'm sorry, Alyn. There was an incident, an accident. She was injured.'

'Is she . . .'

Felix closed his eyes and nodded sadly. 'I'm sorry, Alyn.'

Alyn shut his eyes tight together. 'Maybe there was a mistake. Maybe she's still . . .'

'She's not. I've been assured it was very quick. Painless.'

'I don't believe it,' Alyn spluttered. 'I don't believe she's gone.'

Felix walked over to the door. 'This is difficult for me too, Alyn, believe me. We never imagined something like this would happen. I regret it terribly.' With that, he surrendered a sympathetic smile and left the room.

Alyn sat in the shower, with his arms wrapped round his knees. The hiss and drone of the water seemed to echo the deadened, hollow feeling inside his chest.

He sat passively for over an hour before staggering to his feet and gripping the glass with wrinkled thumbs.

After getting dressed, he found Felix reading a newspaper in the kitchen.

'I need your word that you won't hurt my friends,' Alyn said.

Felix lowered the newspaper and studied Alyn over his glasses.

'And I need the other kids in the prison freed. As soon as possible. I need them all returned to their families.'

'They were always going to be returned eventually, Alyn,' Felix answered.

'If you want me to help you, I need your word,' Alyn said. 'I need you to promise me.'

Felix smiled. 'I knew you'd come round eventually.'

36

Jes and Ryan had both been asleep in the back of the car for the past few hours. As they drifted round a corner, Ryan slowly opened his eyes to find Jes's head on his shoulder.

Jes murmured softly as he looked out of the window. The fields were bleached by snow and a stream of swirling flakes flowed endlessly at the windows.

Without thinking, Ryan turned his neck and kissed her forehead.

'Huh?' Jes said, half asleep.

Ryan froze and shut his eyes, pretending to be asleep.

Jes sat up, rubbing her eyes. 'Where are we?' she asked.

'Still a long way to go. Gotta take the scenic route in case the Pledge are watching the motorways,' Charlie said. He pushed his cap to the side. 'Get some rest while you can.'

'I don't think Stephen's going to call back,' Harlan grumbled, looking at the telephone box. 'So much for your plan, Julian.'

'He'll call,' Julian said. He shivered, pulling his knees close to his chest. They'd spent another night sleeping rough, taking turns to keep an eye on the phone. Other than the name 'Felix', which could be anyone, this was their only concrete lead and Julian wasn't prepared to let it go so soon.

As he was considering this, the phone in the telephone box rang. 'So much for my plan?' Julian said, looking pleased with himself. 'Now do you want to get that or shall I?'

Harlan nodded towards the phone.

'Yes?' Julian said, lifting the receiver to his ear. 'Who is it?'

'I think you know,' said a voice, clearly upper-class and smooth in its diction. 'You have something of mine.'

Harlan snatched the telephone from Julian. 'Are you behind it? Your company's name was on the ibis –'

Julian elbowed him and pulled the telephone out of his hands. 'My *colleague* means that we have something to discuss with you.'

'Oh?'

'We want you to meet us here,' Julian said. 'Within an hour. Alone.'

'Or?'

'Or your precious weapon will go straight to the highest bidder. By this time next week there'll be a hundred clones. Considering how advanced this thing is, I'd say it'll cost you a few billion in contracts . . .'

'An interesting offer,' the voice answered, giggling. 'But I'll do one better – you come to me.'

Harlan pulled the telephone back from Julian. 'No way. We do this out in the open.'

'Oh. There might be a problem with that,' the voice said. 'I've already sent some of my people to collect you. In fact, they should probably be arriving as we speak.'

Harlan looked up. Three men hurried out of the rear of a white van, parked a short distance away from them.

'It's a set-up! He must've traced the call –'

He dropped the telephone and pushed the door open but Julian grabbed the handle.

'We'll never outrun them from here,' Julian said. Over his shoulder another pair appeared from a second van on the other side of the road, surrounding them. 'Quick, help me hold it shut . . .'

Harlan grabbed the handle. One of the men tapped the glass phone box menacingly and waved to them. He tried pulling the door open, but Harlan and Julian managed between them to hold it shut.

The rest of the men arrived, encircling the phone box.

One of the gang yanked the door hard, with enough force to create a gap. He reached inside, grabbing at Julian's coat. Harlan removed his ibis and fired at the grasping hand.

The man yowled and fell away, his arm hanging limp. Each of the gang began slamming their fists at the glass, beating it over and over. The panes rattled. The beats grew rhythmic and began to synchronize into a steady drum.

Another man, taller and broader than the others, pushed his way to the front and pulled hard at the door.

'I'm losing my grip!' Julian announced, trying his best to secure it. Harlan held the bar in two hands, leaning back. With each pull from the other side, the gap between the door and the side of the cubicle grew wider.

Julian was about to let go of the handle entirely when they both heard the sound of a car screeching across the pavement. The men outside turned their heads as one.

'Now!' Julian threw himself at the door, knocking two of the distracted men off balance and giving him and Harlan the chance to make a break through the rest.

'*After them!*' yelled one of the men. Three set off in pursuit, but the silver sports car sped in front, blocking their path.

Anton leant out of the window and yelled, 'Harlan, Julian! Get in!' He spun the steering wheel in their direction and the car bounced over the pavement after them.

'He knows our names!' Julian panted, trying to keep up with Harlan. He stopped and turned as the car raced past them.

The back door was flung open. 'Get in, will you?' said an impatient Pyra.

The pair looked behind at the men who were hurtling towards them.

'It's the car or *them*,' Harlan said. He ran to the car and threw himself inside.

Julian stood in the road, watching helplessly as the gang were almost upon him.

'Julian!' Harlan cried from inside the car. 'Are you getting in or what?'

Julian snapped out of his trance. He rushed towards the car and dived inside, slamming the door shut just as a hand was centimetres from grabbing his leg.

Several of the gang members raced back towards their van and it soon set off in pursuit of the Guild's car. They tore round the corner and over the pavement, knocking a bin on its side. In the back of the car, Harlan and Julian were slammed together into the door, and then were thrown back the other way. The floor of the car trembled as Anton increased the pressure on the accelerator, pulling far ahead of their pursuers.

As Harlan managed to disentangle himself from Julian in the back of the car, he felt a familiar prodding on the back of his shoulder. 'Elsa?'

'Hello,' she said with a smile.

'Oh great,' Julian mumbled.

Elsa flung her arms round the pair. 'So glad to see you both,' she said. 'I'm sorry I left . . . I just . . . I didn't know what to do.'

'You can start by letting go of me,' said a breathless Julian, slipping out of her arms.

'What are you doing here?' Harlan panted. 'Who are *they*?'

'We picked her up en route to her parents' house,' Pyra said. 'It was a stupid idea for her to go back there when there are people like *that* looking for you. What were you thinking, letting her go like that?'

'You think we didn't try telling her? It's like speaking to a brick wall,' Julian said, sighing theatrically. He rapped the side of Elsa's head. 'Sometimes I wonder if there's anything in that head of hers at all.'

'Ow, get off,' Elsa said, and swatted his hand away. 'Anyway, you two got yourselves in trouble too!'

'Harlan's fault,' Julian cut in quickly. 'If he hadn't given the game away by interrupting on the telephone, Stephen might've believed me.'

'It was *your* plan,' Harlan argued. 'I told you it was stupid.'

'What happened to you two anyway?' Elsa said to Harlan.

Harlan opened his mouth to speak, but then looked at Pyra and Anton.

'It's OK,' Elsa said. 'They're on our side.'

Harlan looked unconvinced. 'You sure we can trust them?'

'You can't be sure of anything,' said Anton. 'But if you'd rather go with the lunatics back there . . . ?'

'Decisions, decisions,' Julian mumbled.

'Julian's ibis broke and we spotted the company's name was written inside,' Harlan reluctantly explained.

'We figured they were probably involved in the whole thing. The company is called SIGIL. They specialize in cutting-edge technology. They're owned by Stephen Nover, the billionaire. We tried coaxing him out.'

'And we just saw how that turned out,' Pyra replied.

'Now,' said Julian, leaning forward, 'is someone going to explain what's going on?'

'We can do stuff,' Elsa exclaimed. 'We have this *Ability* –'

'I thought I told you not to say anything, Elsa,' Pyra interrupted.

Elsa went on regardless. 'We can make things happen by using our imagination. Pretty cool, huh?'

'*Make things happen?*' Julian said, narrowing his eyes. 'Have you been dropped on your head or something?'

Elsa shook her head. 'It's real, Julian! I'm not lying.'

'Well, *I* don't understand,' Julian said. 'And I'm the smartest one here, so obviously it doesn't make sense.'

'It's the *only* thing that makes sense,' Harlan murmured. 'My whole life I've felt like I've been surrounded by patterns . . . coincidences.'

'This is insane,' Julian argued. 'You can't honestly believe this.'

'I said the same thing,' Anton offered. 'We all did. But we can prove it.'

He made sure they weren't being followed and pulled the car down a quiet suburban road and parked at the kerb. A boy was playing with a remote-controlled car on the snow-edged pavement.

'Make the car crash,' Pyra said. 'All three of you, use your imagination together.'

Harlan, Elsa and Julian all looked at the toy car zipping quickly over the icy pavement.

'See?' said a sceptical Julian. 'Nothing's happening . . .'

'Shush!' Pyra looked back at them. 'Really imagine it. Make it so vivid that it looks real.'

Harlan took a deep breath and shut his eyes. He visualized the car spinning out of control and crashing with such concentration that Julian's sighs next to him melted away until he was totally absorbed in his imagination. A tingling sensation began in his forehead and increased in intensity. The boy continued pressing the remote control with his thumb, and sneezed suddenly. Inadvertently nudging the steering wheel, he looked up just in time to see the car careering towards an oncoming real one. He gasped and yanked the control in the opposite direction. The toy car hit a patch of ice, spun wildly and cartwheeled against the kerb.

Harlan opened his eyes to find Elsa staring at the toy car, her mouth hanging open in disbelief. Julian was leaning forward, baffled. He turned to Harlan, who was also speechless.

The boy ran over to the toy car, which was upside down with its wheels still spinning. As he lifted it up, a piece of the plastic bumper clattered to the ice.

Harlan put a hand to his head. 'This is a huge amount of responsibility,' he said quietly, feeling a row of goose pimples prickle the back of his neck.

'That's where *we* come in,' Anton said. 'To train you. To make sure you use it properly.'

This can't be possible, Julian thought. *It's just a coincidence. We didn't make that car crash. We couldn't have done.* He watched the boy examine his broken car, unable to take his eyes away. A cocktail of dread and nausea began to curdle in his stomach.

'You OK, Julian? You've gone really pale,' Elsa said.

'It's not real,' he said. 'It's a mistake. It's not real, it's not real . . .'

'Julian, what the hell's the matter with you?' said Harlan. 'You just saw it –'

'Let me out,' he said. 'Please, I'm . . . I'm going to be sick.'

Julian clambered out over Harlan and fell on to the pavement, coughing and retching.

'What's the matter with him?' Pyra said. 'Weird kid.'

Harlan pulled off his seatbelt and went outside to Julian. 'I know it's a shock, but I'm sure they'll explain everything . . .'

Julian looked up, panting. 'Get away from me. Get away.'

Elsa poked her head out of the window. 'Come on, Julian, we've got to head back . . . They're going to train us –'

'I'm not going anywhere with them. Leave me alone.'

He pushed Harlan's hand away, got to his feet and sprinted along the street.

'Damn it,' Pyra said, tearing off her seatbelt and kicking open the door. 'Julian, you need to come back! It's not safe!'

She chased after him, but by the time she reached the next road, Julian was long gone.

37

Ten years ago

Julian's aunt sighed and turned up the television as her six-year-old nephew lay sprawled beside the couch. He clutched the red car and made a throaty engine noise, dragging it in a swooping arc with his hand across the carpet.

'For the love of . . .' his aunt muttered and switched positions, thrusting the remote control at the television. 'No wonder your parents wanted a chance to get out. Next time I'll charge them for this,' she muttered.

Julian, quite oblivious to his aunt's distress, grabbed a white car with his other hand and smashed them together, forcing an explosion sound from his lips. 'Crash!' he squealed. 'Did you see that? I made them crash!'

'*Julian!*'

Julian stopped. He gently placed the cars side by side. 'Didn't have to shout,' he said, pouting, and rolled on to his back.

'Actually I did. Can't you do something a bit quieter?'

He shook his head.

'Then at least go outside, will you? I'm trying to watch something.'

Julian looked down at the cars, then up at his aunt.

'I mean it,' she said, pointing at the door to the hallway. She held her finger outstretched until Julian eventually skulked outside with his toy cars. She reached over for her glass of wine.

Almost an hour passed and Julian's sound effects were little more than a faint hum in the hall beneath the chattering television. After another few glasses of wine, his aunt had gradually unspooled across the couch.

'What ... what is it?' she grumbled, feeling Julian tugging at her jumper. Not realizing she had fallen asleep, she found the empty wine glass lying across her stomach.

'There's someone at the door,' Julian said, tapping her.

His aunt closed her eyes but was jolted awake again by a series of knocks, rattling the glass on the door pane.

'Ms Drury, please open up!' bellowed a man's voice.

Wearily she gathered herself and plodded outside into the hallway.

'Ouch!' She had trodden on one of Julian's toy cars on its back beside the hallway radiator. She bent down and picked up the car, waving it threateningly in his face. 'Put these away,' she snarled and thrust it towards him. 'You'll end up causing an accident if you're not careful.'

Realizing she still had the television remote in her hand, she dropped it on the stairs and opened the front door.

'Miss Drury?' said the police officer on the doorstep. He was standing with a colleague, a young woman with a serious expression.

'Yes,' she said, eyes flitting between them both. 'What is it?'

'Can we speak with you inside?' the woman said, forcing a smile.

'What's this about?'

'It might be better if we just come in,' said the man.

Julian's aunt turned to find her nephew peeking out from behind the door.

'My nephew's here,' she said. 'I don't want to frighten him.'

'I can sit with him,' said the female officer, insistent.

Eventually Julian's aunt gave a faint nod and stepped to the side. The female police officer stepped in and went straight over to the boy and knelt in front of him. 'Those are nice cars. Can I have a look? Which is your favourite?' she said, then led him to the kitchen out of earshot.

Julian's aunt turned away from her nephew and looked at the man standing in front of her.

'Miss Drury, I said *there's been an accident,*' said the

police officer. 'Would you like to take a seat?' he went on. 'Maybe if we go inside . . .'

She sank on to the stairs and put her hands neatly on her lap.

'It was involving your sister and your brother-in-law,' he said. 'Is that their son? Julian?'

His aunt peered through the banisters. Julian was sitting in the kitchen at the table, while the female police officer sat at his side, moving the cars back and forth.

'There's been a terrible accident on the motorway. I'm so sorry.'

'Both . . . of them?'

'Yes,' he said after a breath. 'Both of them.' He continued to speak but his words dampened and dulled. Julian's aunt wordlessly watched her nephew through the banisters, playing with his cars on the table, and at that moment he looked up and waved. With tears clouding her eyes, she slowly lifted her hand and waved back.

38

After returning to the Guild's base minus Julian, Elsa sprang out of the car and beckoned to Harlan to follow her. Harlan warily climbed out as Anton parked, and looked up with a growing suspicion at the dilapidated block of flats.

'This way,' Elsa said.

Harlan stepped over a dead bird and followed her to the entrance. Elsa jabbed in the key code Pyra had taught her and pulled open the gated door.

As soon as the lift arrived on the top floor, Harlan stepped out, gazing around at the ornate cream-coloured ceiling, the stone columns and the tiled floor. 'Look at this place,' he said. 'It's like a temple or something . . .'

His footsteps echoed as he followed Elsa around the room, unable to shake the sensation that the entire thing might be a dream.

'Yep,' Elsa said. She dragged him to one of the windows and made him look out. 'They've even graffitied the side of it to keep people away!' She pointed to an illegible scrawl on the floor below. 'And see that?' she pointed to another window, which showed a cluttered kitchen with a sink full of dirty crockery. 'It's a painting! No one has a clue this place is here.'

Before Harlan had chance to take it all in, Elsa grabbed his arm and pulled him away from the window. 'This is my friend, Harlan!' Elsa shouted to the few other members who were sitting on a leather couch by the wall. They all looked up and waved, except a white-haired man who was jabbing furiously at a laptop.

'I haven't learned their names yet,' she whispered behind her hand.

'How do you think they afforded this place?' Harlan murmured, gazing at the enormous star on the tiled floor, then back up to the coffered ceiling.

She shrugged. 'Probably used the Ability to win the lottery or something.'

'Yeah . . .' Harlan said, his voice trailing off. 'Maybe they did.'

After showing Harlan the gymnasium, library and dining room, an excitable Elsa took Harlan to the sleeping quarters. 'You'll be staying here,' she said, opening the door to a room with a pair of bunk beds. On the lowest bed of one were some folded clothes.

'Can't wait to get out of this uniform.' Harlan grinned, sniffing himself. At that moment, a woman with short blonde hair appeared behind the pair.

'Luthan wants to see you both on the roof,' she said. 'So you can start your training.'

*

'Just two of you?' Luthan emerged on to the roof of the tower block, watched by a waiting Elsa and Harlan. He wore a red scarf tucked into his overcoat and a pair of leather gloves. 'I thought there was supposed to be another.'

'So did we,' said Elsa, shrugging. 'He did a runner on the way here. He got freaked out, I think.'

Luthan nodded and looked over the edge of the roof. 'Let's hope we can find him before the Pledge do. It isn't safe out there, and I fear your friend might be in danger.' He looked back at the pair. 'You both know why you're here, don't you?'

'You're training us,' Harlan said.

'Correct. I'm training you. Now,' he said, presenting three fingers, 'there are three levels in the Guild before we can accept you as a full member. To progress you need to pass a series of tests. Whether you're trying to influence the laws of physics, the behaviour of another, or even yourselves, the mechanics of the Ability are more or less the same throughout. We start small and work our way up.'

Harlan and a slightly distracted Elsa both nodded in unison.

Luthan reached into his pocket and removed two silver coins. He gave one to each of them. 'I want you to flip the coin and try to influence it to land on its edge.'

'The edge?' Harlan said. 'It's barely a couple of millimetres . . .'

'It's impossible!' Elsa declared at the same time.

'You'll need to start changing your beliefs about

what's possible if you're ever going to succeed,' Luthan said.

Harlan and Elsa looked at one another and shrugged. Both coins sailed a short way above them and landed flat.

'Try again.'

Elsa threw her coin up and watched as it quickly descended and clinked against the roof. 'Crap. I'm no good at this . . .'

'Don't be ridiculous, Elsa,' said Harlan. 'You've only tried twice.'

'And failed twice.' She flipped the coin again and waited for the inevitable conclusion. 'Look, it's tormenting me!'

'You need to train your imagination until it feels razor sharp. You should feel it *jolt* you. Now try again . . .'

Elsa threw the coin high into the air and shut her eyes. In a sudden movement Luthan removed a knife from inside his coat and pressed it against her throat. 'Do it,' he hissed.

The sensation of the cold metal blade pressed against Elsa's throat paralysed her into compliance. She visualized the coin standing on its edge in her mind's eye, terrified to take her concentration from it.

She opened her eyes just as the coin hit the ground and rolled a short distance on its side. An odd, yet not unfamiliar, tingling sensation flooded her mind as the coin continued to roll and eventually stopped.

Elsa freed herself from Luthan's grip, holding her throat. 'Maniac!' she spluttered.

'Oh, come on, I wasn't really going to cut you.' He put the knife away, knelt and pointed at the standing coin. 'Nothing focuses the mind quite like fear, Elsa.'

'Why are we even doing this?' she said with a sigh. 'Flipping a coin? What good is that? Waste of time . . .'

'We start with something small,' Harlan answered. 'That's what this is.'

'Correct!' Luthan patted Harlan's shoulder enthusiastically. 'We start small. Whether it's influencing the air currents to make a coin land on its side, or the synapses between someone's brain cells to implant a thought or memory, or even nudging gravity to help win at a roulette table. When you're old enough to play on one, of course,' he added with a smile. 'It doesn't matter. The principles are always the same. Get practising, and soon you'll get a feeling for how to tap into it.'

Luthan soon left to let the pair practise by themselves. After half an hour of flipping the coin, Harlan found his imagination increasing to the point where he could see the glint of sunlight on the coin's corrugated silver edge and the smear of shadow on the gravel beneath.

'Think I've got the hang of it,' he said, watching intently as the coin wobbled gently and stabilized itself for a third time.

Elsa looked on with envy. 'Stupid thing won't work for me.'

'It'll come with practice. Try not to beat yourself up.'

'Baldy knows I'm rubbish,' she said. 'Fat lot of good it'll do me if it only works when there's a knife at my throat . . .'

'Hey, aren't you excited by all of this, Elsa?' Harlan said, smiling. 'I mean, we've found out we can alter reality!'

'Maybe the only reality I want to alter is the one where I'm stuck here when I could be at home instead,' she mumbled. She flipped the coin up again and sighed.

Harlan gazed at the city below. 'You could be home right now, watching television or getting ready for school. But you're not; you're a part of something *huge*. Who would've thought that all these forces were at work, pulling the world in different directions?'

'Probably explains why everything's so messed up at the moment. I'm glad you're enjoying it anyway.' She tossed the coin up a final time and let it fall to the floor.

'Come on, Elsa,' Harlan said. 'I know they want us to learn the basics first, but let's try something a bit more fun. You and me. We focus on it together, all right?'

Harlan hopped on to the edge of the roof. Wind blew frantically at his hair, tearing it in all directions. He removed a ten-pound note from his pocket and folded it into a paper aeroplane.

'Please don't tell me you're gonna waste that, Harlan.'

Harlan scrutinized his creation, shrugging. 'There'll be more where it came from. Let's try to make it catch fire.' He grinned, and before Elsa had the chance to protest, launched the aeroplane off the roof.

Elsa watched as it sailed gently through the air. 'How are we supposed to make it catch fire?' she said. 'They've already told us we shouldn't do anything crazy –'

'Just use your imagination,' Harlan said, shutting his eyes.

Elsa closed her eyes too and visualized the paper aeroplane smouldering and blackening as fire chewed through its wings. She held the image in her mind for at least a minute, and when she opened them, the paper plane was still floating idly through the air.

See? she very nearly said. *It doesn't work* – before noticing it was being swept along on another air current. The plane looped, then plummeted quickly towards the ground. Elsa noticed a pair of women outside the entrance to the adjacent tower block, lighting up cigarettes. The plane changed direction again and seemed to turn from its course, then swooped again towards the pair.

'Look!' she exclaimed. Harlan opened his eyes just in time to see it veer into the path of the lighter. One of the women yelped as the plane flew through the flame, catching a spark on its wing, which quickly spread.

'We did it!' Harlan said, hopping down from the wall.

'Where are you going? You're not just leaving me up here, are you?'

'I have something I need to do,' he called across as he walked away.

'They won't let you out,' Elsa said. 'We're not allowed

to leave by ourselves – they think we'll get caught. They have someone standing guard down there.'

'Think you can distract them for me?'

Elsa looked unsure. 'If they find out, we'll be in trouble.'

'*Please*, Elsa? I'll owe you one.'

39

'We have some problems,' said Felix. 'Internal ones. And that's where I think you could really help.'

Alyn had just slipped into a navy suit with a pale blue tie. He tugged at the collar, which felt as though it was strangling him.

'You said this was for the greater good,' Alyn replied. 'So why am I getting involved in all this stuff?'

'The way the Pledge operates,' Felix explained, 'is through *wealth*. Whoever has the most money leads. There were really only ever two candidates in the running for leadership. Me and Stephen Nover.'

'I know him,' Alyn said. 'Had to watch a documentary about him in school.'

Felix seemed somewhat amused. 'And what did you take from it?'

Alyn shrugged. 'If you're born rich, you'll probably only get richer.'

'I recommend you never say that to his face.' Felix smiled, straightening Alyn's tie. 'He's easily offended. If I could convince Antonia and Blythe to vote together, we could block him from becoming leader. Despite the smiling photographs and all the charity donations, Stephen is a deeply unbalanced young man, with a particularly nasty streak.'

'So why don't they just vote against him?'

'Fear,' Felix replied.

'And you want me to help you change their minds. But I don't even know what I'm supposed to do,' Alyn said. 'I don't know anything about this *Ability* . . .'

'Because you haven't yet been trained to use it. All you need to do is be there when I meet with Antonia and Blythe and use your imagination to *make* them agree. You'll know when it's worked. You might feel a little woozy.'

Alyn took a step closer to Felix, narrowing his eyes. 'If I find out you're using me, we're through. And I swear I'll see to it that you're brought to justice.'

'You care about your friends, don't you?' Felix said, as Alyn began to walk away. Alyn stopped and turned back. 'Then do this for their sakes. Stephen will do anything for power, including *murder*. If he takes control, none of you are safe.'

Alyn sat cross-legged by the window in Felix's luxury penthouse apartment later that afternoon, gazing at the city below, already illuminated as the winter sun dipped in the overcast sky. The floorboards were cold against his ankles. He made a circle shape with his fingers and peered through it, focusing on a row of lights in an office block.

'Turn off,' he whispered, and waited, watching the lights.

Almost a minute passed and nothing had happened. He then pictured the lights turning off, and held the thought.

Imagination, Felix had told him.

Alyn remembered something he'd read in a book once, that the smallest cause could create an effect of catastrophic proportions. The example was a butterfly flapping its wings on one side of the world and causing a tsunami on the other.

Conjuring the image of a black butterfly in his mind's eye, Alyn pictured it fluttering past him, through the window and soaring on the wind, spiralling down to the office building. He visualized the butterfly passing through the wall and into the electrical circuits. At that moment the lights in the office went out.

Alyn sat up straight, staring at the single row of darkened windows.

40

'Hey!' Elsa called down from her bedroom window to the Guild member who was guarding the gated door at the entrance to the tower block. 'Yeah, you down there on the wall . . .'

The man, whose long blond hair was tumbling beneath his woolly hat, looked up at her over his shoulder. 'What d'you want?'

'I'm bored. I want to go for a walk,' Elsa called down. Harlan, waiting on the ground floor on the other side of the door, peered out from round the corner.

'Well, you can't,' the man grumbled, folding his arms. 'You 'ave to stay.'

Come on, Elsa, Harlan thought. *You can do better than that*.

'Baldy was trying to teach me the coin thing,' she went on. 'But I'm no good!'

'Practise!' the man called back wearily. He unscrewed a bottle of water and took a sip.

Seconds later, the guard yelped and grabbed his head. 'What did you just throw at me?'

'Sorry!' Elsa called back from above. 'It was my coin – can you find it for me?'

He muttered at her and got up from the low wall. Harlan took this as his opportunity to creep towards the door. The guard turned away from Harlan and hunched over, looking for Elsa's coin.

'I see it!' Elsa yelled down. 'It's right there, by the drain! No, not there, a bit to the right . . .'

Harlan looked up at Elsa, gave her a thumbs-up, and scurried across the grass.

He walked until he found a shabby-looking amusement arcade, less than a mile away, sandwiched between an off-licence and a launderette. Harlan stepped inside, gazing around at the pulsing lights, and eventually settled on a fruit machine by the door.

He inserted a couple of coins and pressed the glowing buttons. *Can't think of a better place to practise*, he thought. As the three reels spun in unison, Harlan shut his eyes.

Inside the machine, the smallest, barely noticeable fluctuation in gravity caused the first reel to falter and slow, and seconds later it landed on the image of a bell.

Harlan felt a tingling sensation inside his skull. He opened his eyes just as the second and third reels also landed on bells. The lights flashed and a cascade of coins clattered into the tray.

This is addictive, he thought, the tingling sensation only just fading. What else might he be able to influence? There seemed no end of possibilities.

'How old did you say you were again?' said the manager, carefully scrutinizing Harlan half an hour later.

'Eighteen,' Harlan lied, scooping the coins from his jumper on to the counter. 'I'd like to change this into notes.'

The manager of the arcade narrowed his eyes and watched Harlan carefully. With a sigh, he reluctantly counted the coins and removed some notes from the till before thrusting them at Harlan. 'If I find out you're cheating . . .' he said, and trailed off as Harlan turned and left.

A few miles from the amusement arcade, not far from where he'd left the Guild's car, Julian perched in a shop doorway, staring vacantly as the rain pattered steadily across the cobblestones. The canvas awning above his head bulged and heaved, and a single trail of water dribbled into a pool beside him.

'*There* you are,' Harlan said, sitting beside Julian. 'It's taken me ages to find you.'

Julian remained silent.

'Come with us,' Harlan said. 'The Guild will look after us. We'll be safe with them – they'll train us, and you'll learn things you never thought were possible . . .'

Only then did Julian turn his head to meet Harlan's eyes. 'This Ability . . . if it's true, it's dangerous. It's a *curse*.'

'Maybe you're right, but that's why we need to learn to use it,' Harlan said excitedly. 'So we can control it. Otherwise –'

Julian looked away. 'For all we know, this whole thing is just another lie.'

'I don't think you really believe that.'

'I might. You don't know anything about me, Harlan.'

'I know you're not as complex as you think you are. You're like the rest of us. A little more selfish perhaps. But in the end, we're not really that different. We've all been thrown into something that we're trying to make sense of.'

'Then why do you even care whether or not I join you and the rest of those weirdos?'

'Where else are you going to go? Back home? What'll you do when *they* come looking for you?'

'I'll manage.'

Harlan smiled. 'You don't even have any money since Elsa stole it.'

'Then I'll sleep here,' Julian said with a shrug. 'I'll find food. I'll survive. It's what I do best.'

'At least give the Guild a try. No one's forcing you to stay.'

'The Guild.' He laughed and shook his head. 'You really think they're any better than the ones who put us in the prison?'

'Anyone's better than them,' Harlan said. He got up and pointed in the direction of the Guild's base. 'It's a grey tower block called Hermes House, twenty minutes away.' Harlan pointed to a couple of faint buildings in the distance. 'If you change your mind – and I hope you do – that's where you'll find us.'

Before he left, Harlan reached inside his pocket and removed a wad of money, at least two hundred pounds. 'You wanted your money back. Here. Take it,' he said, and passed it to Julian.

Julian looked baffled. 'Where did you get it? Why are you doing this?'

'Looking out for you,' Harlan said. 'How else are you going to learn, Julian?' He said nothing else and walked away quickly through the falling rain.

41

After a long afternoon of practising unsuccessfully with the coin, Elsa hopped up from her bed and walked over to the window. *Wish they'd give me something a little more exciting to do*, she thought, sighing, turning the coin between her fingers. At this rate, she'd never be a proper member of the Guild, not if she couldn't pass the most basic test.

She left the bedroom and paused by the locked door at the end of the corridor. Elsa made sure nobody was looking and edged slowly towards it. It was as though something was pulling her and she was unable to resist.

She took a final step and peered through the keyhole. She was sure there was something in there, a shape. But what . . . ?

Pyra grabbed her by the arm, pulling her away. 'Thought you were told to stay away from that room. You have trouble listening to orders?'

'Nope,' said Elsa, 'I just have trouble obeying them.'

Pyra narrowed her eyes. 'I have something to do. Want to come? Keep you out of trouble!'

Elsa shrugged. 'Depends, I guess. What kind of thing?'

'Surveillance,' Pyra clarified.

'You're spying on someone? Who?'

'His name's Lord Blythe. He's a close associate of James Felix. The two have been hanging around a lot recently.' She lifted a rolled-up newspaper in her hand and opened it to a picture of a suspicious-looking Blythe and Felix. 'The papers think they're involved in some dodgy business merger, but thanks to what you told us about Felix, we think it might be about the Pledge.'

Elsa studied the picture for a few moments. 'How are you going to find this Blythe guy?'

'He's not as secretive as Felix,' Pyra said. 'The opposite in fact.'

'And you want me to help you *spy* on him?'

'Sure. I think it might do you some good. Come on.'

Pyra pulled her away as Elsa looked at the locked door one last time.

Half an hour later, the pair were standing together on the crowded tube. Pyra was leaning against a pole with her arms folded, while Elsa squinted at the tube map.

'How are you finding the training?' Pyra asked. Elsa looked up.

'Hard, I guess. I've done everything Baldy told me.'

'And?'

'I'm not good enough. I don't think I'll ever do it. I can imagine what I'm supposed to; I just can't concentrate.'

Pyra slipped a hand inside her jeans pocket and removed the domino. 'It's called a locus,' she said.

Elsa took the domino with her forefinger and thumb, examined it and dropped it back in Pyra's hand. 'Can I have one?'

'You need to get your own. It works best if it means something to you. It doesn't even need to be an actual *thing*. It could be a symbol, a word, a memory . . . If you're trying to influence things, your own desire can sometimes get in the way. A locus can help you concentrate.'

'A blue elephant,' Elsa said, a little embarrassed. 'It's my favourite toy. My parents used to put it on the floor by my bed when I was sleeping. They said it'd keep the monsters away. After a while, I didn't even need the toy when I was scared, I just used to think of it. Can I use that as my locus?'

'Knock yourself out. Anyway, this is our stop,' Pyra said, and headed on to the train platform.

Elsa struggled to keep up as they went up a flight of stairs to the escalators. She gazed at the advertisements floating past them on either side. 'So where do we find this Blythe guy then?'

'There's a little restaurant in Covent Garden,' said Pyra. 'Apparently he eats there every Wednesday.'

'So we're just gonna bust in and grab a seat next to him?'

'We're not going to do anything as fun as that. We're going to wait.'

They turned right out of the station and walked past the gathered crowds, who were circled around a few street performers. The scent of cooked food drifted out of the little restaurants and bistros dotted around. Elsa felt her stomach rumble as they entered the piazza.

'Down here,' Pyra said, pointing to a road. 'There's a coffee shop opposite. We can sit there and wait.'

After brushing some raindrops from the metal chairs, the two sat at the table, with Pyra facing the restaurant door on the opposite side of the road. She ordered two coffees for them both and a short while later a smiling waitress emerged with their drinks.

'You haven't told me how you got involved with the Guild,' Elsa said.

'Was I supposed to?'

'No, I was just wondering. That's all.'

'I've been in and out of care my whole life,' said Pyra after a moment's pause. 'When I started to realize about the Ability I wasn't all that much older than you. They told me I was sick.'

'But you weren't, right?'

'Well, I might've been,' said Pyra. 'I was an angry kid. Got into a bit of trouble and had to stay at a young offenders' institution. On my last night there, I imagined it burning to the ground. Three days later, it did. They said it was a mix of things – a dodgy plug, some turpentine that hadn't been cleaned up properly, old batteries in the smoke alarm. No one person's fault . . .'

'But you were the spark? At least that's what you think, right?'

Pyra went to speak but cut herself short and shrugged. 'I dunno. But that's why *we* exist . . . to train people, so we can take control of it, and use it for *good*.' Her eyes swept quickly past Elsa to the restaurant door. 'Anyway, look. That's our man.'

Elsa spun round in her chair, but Pyra grabbed her wrist. 'Don't make it so obvious,' she said. 'You think that your training is all about using the Ability, but there's a lot more to it than that.' She waited until Blythe was a short distance away and stood still. 'Come on, follow me.'

42

'So,' said Alyn, as the chauffeur-driven car weaved through streams of afternoon traffic, 'who's first?'

'The lowest-ranking member of the Pledge. His name is Blythe.'

'Does it ever bother you that you might be cheating?' Alyn said.

'Cheating? Not at all,' Felix chuckled. 'Had you found Stephen, he'd have had you do the same, I'm sure. The boy doesn't like me at all, for some reason or another.'

Alyn watched Felix clean his glasses on a silk handkerchief. 'So while you and Blythe are talking, I have to imagine him agreeing to kick Stephen out,' Alyn said. 'That's all.'

'It's not as simple as just imagining, Alyn. You have to focus with every fibre of your being, as though you're forcing your imagination to replace reality itself.'

It was easier switching off some lights, Alyn pondered. *Manipulating someone's thoughts seems like something else.*

'And afterwards,' Felix added, 'I'll take you out for a burger. What do you say?'

Alyn followed Felix out of the car to a large Edwardian townhouse. Standing outside was an overweight grey-haired man with a moustache and a reddened face, a cigar planted between his fingers like a paintbrush.

'Blythe,' said Felix, extending his hand. 'It's good to see you.'

'Likewise,' Blythe announced. He turned his scrutiny to Alyn.

'I want you to meet my apprentice,' Felix said. 'This is Alyn.'

Blythe let his cigar droop and tilted back his neck. 'Ah yes,' he murmured, billowing a stream of smoke. 'Poor chap, whatever did you do to deserve this? He's working you to the bone, I'll bet!' Blythe slapped a heavy hand on Alyn's arm and laughed loudly.

'Is there somewhere we can talk in private?' Felix asked.

'Indeed.' Blythe took another pull on his cigar, and steered them both away from the front steps. 'Follow me.'

Alyn braced himself for another enthusiastic pat on his shoulder and followed the two men until they arrived at a prestigious hotel at the bottom of the next street. An attentive pudgy-faced doorman stood rigid, hands clasped neatly behind his back. Overhead a white flag rippled and fluttered in the cold air.

'Good afternoon, gentlemen,' the doorman said, recognizing the pair and stepping aside.

Elsa peeped out from round the wall, squinting at them.

'They've gone inside that hotel!' she whispered to Pyra. 'There was someone else with them too, but I couldn't really see. You think we should follow them?'

Pyra looked down at her torn jeans and leather jacket. 'Not *we*. You.'

'But I can't –'

'Time to stop thinking about what you can't do, Elsa, and focus on what you *can*. This is all part of your training . . . using your wits and learning to think on your feet. Luthan is a traditionalist. He might have you flipping that coin, but I prefer to get you out there.'

Elsa pulled a face. 'What do I do once I'm inside?'

'Get a cup of hot chocolate and relax.' Pyra smiled. 'I'm kidding, of course. See if you can overhear anything that might be useful. If you feel in danger just leave, I'll be waiting right here.'

Pyra gave Elsa an encouraging shove and slipped back behind the wall. Elsa trotted along the pavement towards the hotel. She felt her stomach sink as she walked through the car park and towards the door.

Blythe sighed. 'Unless I'm mistaken, we've already had this conversation, Felix. You want me and Antonia to join you in voting Stephen out of the Pledge.'

On the far side of the room, Alyn had been struggling

to keep an image in his mind of Blythe agreeing with Felix's request.

'I've heard it all before, and my answer is still the same. He's more use to us *in* than out, and we don't want to upset the applecart. There would be ghastly repercussions if this went ahead.'

'There would be repercussions if it *didn't*,' Felix argued. 'You really see him in charge of the Pledge some day, Blythe? You want everyone's fate in *his* hands – the hands of a madman?'

'Fate is *always* in the hands of madmen, Felix. Because madmen are the only ones cunning enough – or stupid enough – to seek that kind of power in the first place.' He leant in towards Felix, lowering his voice. 'Besides, do you really think this is the time to be discussing such matters? I don't see why you needed to bring *him* along.'

'Alyn has no idea about any of this,' Felix lied, slowly sipping his drink. 'He's just been running some errands for me.'

'Hm. Well, anyway, I need the little boys' room,' Blythe said. 'Another gin and tonic, if you're buying.'

He stood, belched loudly with a look of pride, and waddled towards the stairs.

Felix waited until he was out of sight before striding across to where Alyn was seated. 'It doesn't seem to be working,' Felix spat. 'He's not changed his mind. You have to keep trying, Alyn. I don't know how much longer I can keep him here. There's a charity gala at the opera house on Friday. All of the Pledge will be attending. This is when I plan on announcing Stephen's dismissal. We need Blythe and Antonia to agree by then.'

Alyn sighed, recognizing the disappointment and desperation in the billionaire's voice. If what he said about Stephen was true, it was vital they succeed. But more than that, Felix was one of the few people to have shown him kindness . . . something even his own father hadn't been able to manage.

'I'll keep trying,' Alyn said.

'I know you're more than capable.' Felix patted his shoulder encouragingly and hurried back to his chair, just as Blythe returned.

Elsa darted inside. So far there was no sign of Felix or Blythe anywhere. She walked cautiously around the sweeping hall, glancing at the rows of framed paintings, floral patterned armchairs, dark wood tables, where guests sat stiffly.

I can't screw this up and make a fool out of myself in front of Pyra, she thought. Otherwise, it was likely to be the first and last time she was invited on a mission.

As Elsa entered the lounge, she saw them. Felix and Blythe were sat in front of a grandiose-looking fireplace. She crept nearer, helping herself to a canapé from a parked trolley.

Elsa dropped into a seat a short way from their table and picked up a newspaper, covering her face. Straining her ears, she tried to make out their conversation.

'I hope to see you at the opera house on Friday,' Felix

said after a short while. 'I don't know about you, but I'll be glad to get the whole thing over with.'

The opera house on Friday, Elsa thought. *I wonder what's going on there?*

Felix stood, stretching, and turned to his apprentice. 'We're done here, Alyn,' he said to the boy at the window. 'Did you manage to get all that work done for me?'

Elsa lowered the newspaper, and saw Alyn making his way towards the pair.

'All of it,' Alyn answered.

'*Alyn?*' she said aloud, and quickly brought the newspaper back over her face. *It can't be him.* She waited for a couple of seconds and peered out again. *It was him. What's he doing here?*

'Pleased to have met you,' Alyn said, shaking Blythe's hand.

Elsa's mouth hung open at the sight of her friend dressed in an expensive suit and shaking hands with the very people who had been responsible for their imprisonment.

'The pleasure is all mine,' Blythe chortled. 'Take care now. And you tell me if he works you too hard; I shall have words!'

The three of them walked back to the foyer and parted ways, with a laughing Blythe giving a final wave and heading for the bar.

43

Henry slowly opened his eyes, finding himself enveloped in a blue-tinged darkness. He felt around, finding only cold stone beneath his fingers. As his eyes became accustomed to the lack of light, he saw wisps of silver vapour flowing from his mouth.

'Where am I?' he said aloud, still groggy. 'Someone . . . Is someone there?'

Moments later there was the sound of footsteps and a door opened with a heavy clank.

Henry squinted at the shape in the doorway and managed to pull himself upright.

'You remember me?' Rayner asked, looking down at his prisoner.

Henry nodded as Rayner stepped inside the cell, closing the door behind him.

Henry pushed himself back against the wall. His arms were weak, and his hands were just beginning to feel the ache of arthritis.

Rayner folded his arms. 'Where have the kids gone?'

Henry looked down. He wiped his white beard with his sleeve.

Rayner leant down, grabbing Henry's shirt. 'You'd better start talking,' he growled. 'Or you won't be leaving this room for a long time.'

Henry opened his mouth to speak, but thought better of it.

'Giving me the silent treatment?' said Rayner. 'I'm used to the kids talking a lot sooner.' He contorted his hand so that the joints in his knuckles cracked.

Henry lowered his eyes.

'You don't know what you're interfering with,' Rayner continued.

'I know exactly what I'm interfering with and it's madness,' Henry blurted out.

'We're saving the country from collapsing,' Rayner argued.

'You're not saving anything or anyone except the rich. *The Pledge*, you think they care about anyone else? They're only trying to preserve things so they can keep their power!'

'You don't know anything, old man,' Rayner said. He released Henry's shirt from his grip and stood up.

'They've tricked you,' Henry spat, soothing his throat. 'You're just another pawn, like everyone else here. If you don't stop the project and release those children at once, you have no idea what kind of damage you'll do. Tell me, have any of them started acting strangely yet? Losing their sense of reality?'

Rayner hesitated.

'I thought so,' Henry said. 'Because that's how it'll start.'

'How *what* will start?'

Henry paused, watching Rayner closely. 'You didn't really think you could get away with manipulating reality without any consequences, did you? If you continue this project, the children are all in great danger . . .'

At that moment the door opened. Rayner looked over his shoulder.

'I want to speak to him,' said a female voice from outside the room. 'Alone.'

Rayner looked at Henry, then at the woman. 'I'll be right outside,' he said.

Henry shielded his eyes from the momentary wave of light as Susannah stepped into the room and closed the door behind her.

'Hello, Henry,' she said, smiling. 'It's been a while.'

44

'Why are we stopping?' Jes said. She had been in a trance for the last few hours.

'Cos we're being followed,' Ryan said, leaning between the seats towards Charlie. 'Isn't that right?'

Their driver nodded. A vehicle had been tailing them for ten minutes, and despite Charlie's best efforts to throw off their pursuer, the car still remained.

'We can't have them following us to our building,' Charlie said.

'Couldn't we just use the Ability to crash their car?' asked Jes.

Charlie looked at her. 'On a main road?' He pulled a face. 'Who knows what damage we'd do.'

'So you've got your own building, eh?' Ryan said, watching as the trailing car turned down the same road as them, the hazy rain swirling in its headlights.

'We do,' Charlie answered. 'You'll like it. It's pretty badass.'

Jes was looking at the crucifix dangling from the rear-view mirror.

'Lock your doors,' Charlie said as the car drew nearer.

'I still got this, remember?' Ryan said, tapping his ibis.

The car pulled alongside theirs. The tinted driver's window slowly descended.

'Is there a reason you're following us?' Charlie said.

The driver of the other vehicle said something that neither Ryan nor Jes could hear.

Charlie got out of the driver's seat. 'Stay here,' he said, and hurried outside.

Ryan leant forward in his seat, trying to see. 'Have a look out of your window,' he said. 'I can't see what's going on. Jes? Are you listening to me?'

Ryan glanced over his shoulder, just as Jes grabbed the ibis and sprang out of the door.

'*Jes!*' Ryan hissed.

He watched as Jes hurried towards the other car, leant in through the open window and fired the ibis.

She ran back round to the open door, threw the ibis on to the seat and leapt back inside beside Ryan. 'All right,' she said. 'Let's go!'

Charlie appeared at the rear of the car, rain dripping from the brim of his baseball cap. 'Jes, what the hell are you playing at?' he said. 'He only wanted to tell me the back lights were busted.'

Jes's mouth fell open. 'But I only meant to help us.'

'We need to get out of here,' Charlie said, getting in and driving the car away from the kerb.

45

There was a frenzied cheer as Stephen's black limousine sidled up to the pavement and the door opened. Hidden from view among the crowd, Julian watched as the billionaire stepped out of the back of the car, ignoring his adoring fans until an adviser whispered in his ear that there were cameras following him.

With that, Stephen's demeanour changed. He smiled sweetly and blew kisses several times to the onlookers. 'Thank you,' he announced. 'Thank you to all my *Noverdosers*. You really are the best fans anyone could ask for!'

There was a collective cheer. 'Can't believe they fall for this stupid act,' Julian muttered despairingly as the grinning Stephen walked towards the crowd. He reached out for an autograph book without even bothering to look at the owner, scribbling something quickly and shoving it towards her.

'Will you marry me?' said a flushed teenager with frizzy hair.

'Marry you?' he sneered, momentarily forgetting himself. 'What do you think I am, blind?'

The girl's mouth fell open. Stephen's adviser quickly leant in, whispering something to him.

'Because if I *were* blind I wouldn't see all these other amazing, wonderful fans!' Stephen exclaimed, quickly correcting himself. 'And by marrying one of you, I would deny everyone else the opportunity ... wouldn't I?'

There was another enthusiastic cheer. Even the recipient of his insult breathed a sigh of relief and graciously accepted his signature, clutching the autograph book to her chest.

Julian narrowed his eyes. *Bet you think you're so clever for sending your thugs after us*, he thought.

After a few more hurried autographs, Stephen found himself accepting a notepad that had been thrust towards him. 'There,' Stephen said, and offered the notepad back.

Julian looked up, saying nothing, his face partly covered by the shadow of his hooded parka.

'I don't even get a thank you?' Stephen said. 'Charming ...'

He pushed the notepad towards Julian and snatched another.

'I know who you are,' Julian said quietly. 'I know *what* you've done.'

Only then did Stephen make eye contact with Julian.

'Stephen, please sign this!' squealed a girl, waving a piece of paper in his direction. 'Please, please!'

'The ball's in my court now,' Julian hissed. 'And I only play when I know I can win.'

'Is that so?' Stephen giggled. He leant towards Julian and whispered, 'Someone's mad that I outsmarted him.'

'Outsmarted me? I'm still free, aren't I?' Beneath his cool facade, Julian felt himself tremble with anger.

'For now.' Stephen signed the girl's paper and stepped away from the crowd, then whispered something to his adviser, who raised himself up on tiptoes to catch sight of a disappearing Julian.

'No more autographs,' Stephen declared. 'I have work to do.'

Much to his fans' dismay, Stephen walked away from the crowd, followed by a suited convoy, and headed inside the skyscraper.

46

It was dark when an excitable Elsa returned to the tower block with Pyra.

As they were waiting for the lift in the dingy hallway, the door clicked and Harlan pushed inside, batting the rain out of his coat. He tipped the hood back and noticed the pair a short way ahead of him.

'You sneaked out!' Pyra exclaimed, narrowing her eyes at him, and Harlan jumped. 'We told you to wait here. Are you stupid? There are people still looking for you.'

'I just ... I had some stuff to do.' He unzipped his coat and Elsa noticed a wad of money poking from the inside pocket.

'Did you help him sneak out, Elsa?'

'No, I swear it! I swear I didn't do anything!'

Pyra glared at Harlan. 'Well, don't do it again. You could've been followed or anything. If you have to go out, make sure one of us goes with you. Understood?'

Harlan nodded.

'We were spying on someone!' Elsa said excitedly as he joined them in the lift. 'It was so cool. I sneaked inside a hotel and everything.'

'Nothing would surprise me any more,' Harlan said.

The lift soon arrived at the top floor and Pyra stepped out. 'You should try to get some sleep,' she said to Elsa and Harlan. 'It's been a long day. Training is early tomorrow. And *no* more going out alone.'

'Hey,' Elsa said once Pyra was some way down the corridor and out of earshot. 'Is that your money? Where did you get it?'

'Mind your own business.' Harlan glared at her and walked round the corner.

Elsa hurried after him. 'Did you steal it? Did you rob someone? Tell me, Harlan, tell me –'

'I won it,' he answered. 'If you must know.'

'You've been gambling,' she said. 'You've been using the Ability to cheat.'

'I found somewhere nearby,' he went on nonchalantly. 'Just some little place that let me play without ID. No big deal.'

'So you *were* gambling.'

'No, I was *training*. I thought what better way to practise than to actually use it.' His eyes widened. 'I tripled Julian's money in less than an hour, Elsa!'

'I hope you're not going back there,' Elsa said. 'They'll think you were cheating and I don't want you coming back in a wheelchair.'

Harlan shrugged. He pushed open the door to his room and went quietly inside. He knelt by the bed and shoved some of the money underneath the mattress.

'Can I tell you something, Harlan?' Elsa said.

'I've a feeling you're going to anyway. What's up?'

'While we were spying, I – I saw Alyn,' she said.

Harlan stopped what he was doing and looked at her.

'He was wearing a suit and tie. It's like he's Felix's assistant or something.'

'It can't have been him.'

'It was. I swear it!'

Harlan sat down on the mattress. 'Did he see you?'

Elsa shook her head. 'Nope. And I didn't tell Pyra anything. You think Felix might have brainwashed him?'

'Either that or he's going after Felix himself,' Harlan said, considering the likelihood of this. 'I don't know, Elsa.'

Elsa nodded. 'Anyway, I'd better practise this coin thing if I ever want to impress Baldy . . .'

Harlan looked behind her and cleared his throat.

Elsa glanced over her shoulder. 'Oh crap,' she muttered, seeing Luthan standing beside the open door.

'So *are* you going to impress me?' he said, folding his arms.

'Nope,' Elsa spluttered. 'But Harlan is – he can do the coin thing already – isn't that right, Harlan?'

'I can speak for myself, Elsa.' He turned to Luthan.

'I think I've got it. So what next? When do we start *proper* training?'

'This *is* proper training. If you don't master the basics, you'll never manage some of our more advanced techniques. But, if you think you're ready to be examined, meet me on the roof tomorrow, noon. I'll let you have a few hours of practice first.'

47

Eight members of the Guild were waiting in the central meeting area when Luthan came through the oak doors. Moonlight was gushing through the row of windows.

'I'm glad you could all attend this emergency meeting,' Luthan said, stepping between two pillars. Between them was an easel, presenting an architectural blueprint mounted on a board. 'I thought it was about time we got together.' He removed a photograph from his jacket and pinned it near the top of the board. 'As you all know, this is James Felix. The kids confirmed his involvement in the Pledge after they found his name and number in a phone they stole back at the prison.'

Anton was leaning against one of the stone columns in a tight black T-shirt, torn jeans and a flat cap. He lifted up a picture of Stephen Nover, showing it to the rest of the group and saying, 'The second-wealthiest man in the country – and Harlan and Julian realized his company made the ibis weapon.' He walked over and pinned the photograph beneath the one of Felix.

There was a murmur of interest from the other

members. Pyra raised a photograph of a ruddy-faced Blythe, dressed in a fox-hunting uniform.

'Lord Blythe,' she said. 'Elsa helped me with surveillance as part of her training and, as we expected, Blythe met Felix. But they weren't talking about business . . .'

'They were talking about the Pledge,' Luthan confirmed. 'Blythe is the third richest in the country. Notice a pattern? The fourth richest is Antonia Black, a very secretive heiress.' With that, he showed a photograph of a diminutive woman with a black bob, exiting a limousine. 'We don't know if she has any involvement, but I'd say it's likely. The Pledge is simply based on who has the most money. After all, that's what they value, more than anything.'

'And by that logic, Felix has the most so he's the one in charge,' said the man sitting beside Pyra. 'It's gonna be hard getting to these guys.'

'Indeed.' Luthan clasped his hands behind his back. 'But Pyra has some news for us, don't you?'

'There's a charity gala at the opera house this Friday . . . A performance, then some masquerade party in the ballroom. Felix and Blythe are both going . . . and Nover's funding the majority of the thing so he'll be there.'

'The Pledge together under one roof,' said Anton. 'Looks like we might have to gatecrash this party.'

Luthan pointed to the blueprint, tracing his finger along the labyrinth of lines. 'There are two entrances,' he said. 'The front is where the cameras will be –'

'And the attention-seekers,' Pyra cut in. 'Like the

celebrities. I'll bet that smarmy little idiot Nover won't miss making a dramatic entrance.'

'Pyra and I will find a way in,' said Luthan. 'Too many of us will raise suspicions. The most important thing is that the project is ended and the children freed. And at the moment we don't have a bargaining chip . . . unless we take a hostage.'

'There's going to be cameras and security everywhere,' said a man sat at the table. 'How do you think we'll manage to get a hostage?'

'I'll use the Ability to get one of the Pledge alone . . . and unconscious. We should be able to get them outside with relative ease; after all, we'll just be concerned a fellow guest has had too much to drink and are escorting them to their car.'

'And we'll be in masks, which should make the whole thing a bit easier,' Anton said.

'In masks?' Elsa had sidled over. She looked at the easel and her eyes widened. 'Whoa, are you lot planning something? Can I come?'

'Yeah,' said Pyra, pushing her back outside. '*We* are planning something. And, no, you can't come. Now get lost.'

'Even after I helped you today?' Elsa looked disappointed.

Pyra shoved Elsa back towards her room. 'What part of getting lost don't you understand?'

48

'OK,' said a relieved Felix, as he left Antonia's office, rubbing his hands briskly together. 'I think that went well.'

Alyn had been sitting in a chair in the deserted reception area, using the Ability to influence Antonia to agree with Felix's request.

'Well done,' Felix said, putting an arm round his shoulder.

'I've got a headache,' Alyn said, holding his brow. It was the same sensation he had felt after being made to watch the peculiar films in the prison.

'You've worked hard. You deserve tomorrow morning off.'

Alyn smiled and walked with Felix to the waiting car.

'So what did she say?' Alyn asked when they were inside. 'Did she agree?'

'Not yet,' Felix answered. He adjusted his tie and combed his white hair with his fingertips. 'But she'll give me her answer by tomorrow morning.'

Alyn seemed disappointed. 'I thought she might've

agreed then and there.' *And I can be done with this whole thing.*

'That's not how it works, Alyn. Remember, this is a natural process. It isn't magic. The Ability guides things. Nudges them. It doesn't make things happen out of thin air. Your influence might've helped produce a memory somewhere in the back of her mind. Or perhaps a feeling. Tonight she may find she can't sleep and those feelings play on her mind, and she starts to obsess over them. She keeps thinking about Stephen and what might happen if he takes control of the Pledge . . .'

'And then she talks herself into taking action,' said Alyn. 'But what if you're wrong about this Stephen guy?'

'I'm not wrong about him. Shortly after we formed the Pledge, I had to visit Stephen at his offices. He'd had to make two dozen or so redundancies. No one in their right mind *enjoys* making redundancies, Alyn, it's one of the most difficult and downright unpleasant things you'll ever have to do. Stephen, on the other hand –' Felix lowered his voice – 'filmed every one of them with a hidden camera. I went into his office to give him some papers and he was sat with his feet up on the desk, almost crying with laughter at these videos – videos of grown men and women begging not to lose their jobs – with a box of popcorn in his hands. I knew he was a loose cannon from that moment.'

'You told me there'd be consequences to kicking Stephen out,' Alyn added. 'Dangerous ones. Are you ready for them?'

Felix looked at him. After a moment's pause he nodded. 'Stephen's not the type to let this go easily, Alyn, but, yes, I'm ready.'

'Then in that case, I'm ready too,' Alyn confirmed with a smile. 'As long as you promise the other kids will be released and unharmed, like we agreed.'

The phone rang in Felix's pocket. 'Yes,' he said, answering it. 'What is it?'

As Felix listened, his expression gradually changed to one of delight. 'Yes. Of course. I understand completely. Thank you.'

He ended the call and put the phone back inside his pocket.

'That was Blythe,' he said, smiling broadly. 'He's agreed. Thank you, Alyn. Now we just need Antonia to agree and Stephen will be expelled.'

49

Charlie stepped out of the lift, followed by a cautious Ryan and Jes. The two of them were both gazing around in quiet bewilderment.

'Hey, what is this place?' Ryan whispered to Jes.

'Secret headquarters,' she whispered back. 'Blatantly.'

Ryan nodded, looking impressed. 'Cool.'

A dejected Elsa was skulking in the corridor with her hands in the pockets of her hooded jumper when she spotted them. 'Jes? Ryan?' She ran towards them both, then after a moment of disbelief threw her arms round them. 'I thought you were dead!' she exclaimed. 'We heard a shot – we thought one of you had been hit . . .'

Jes grinned. 'I was. I'd show you the scar but you're . . . kind of crushing it right now.'

Elsa pulled away and grimaced.

'What's going on out here?' asked Harlan, appearing behind them. His eyes widened when he saw Ryan and Jes.

'Great to see you,' he said, putting his arm round

Ryan's shoulder. 'And in one piece too. We didn't think you were coming.'

'We almost weren't,' Ryan said, looking a little embarrassed by the attention. 'So you lot staying here or something?'

'For now,' said Harlan. 'Beats sleeping on the streets – not something I plan on doing again anytime soon . . .'

Ryan looked at Jes. 'And we thought those stinking tunnels were bad.' He sniffed himself. 'I'll never get this smell out.'

'Speaking of bad smells, Julian was supposed to be with us now, but he went a bit weird.' Elsa tapped the side of her head. 'Who knows where he is! Maybe the Pledge has got him.'

'Figures,' Ryan said with a snort. 'So I guess you heard all about this Ability thing or whatever it's called then?'

'And?' Elsa asked. 'What do you think?'

It's a load of crap, Ryan thought, then quickly replied with a dismissive shrug. 'I still don't believe a word of it.' He waited for a response from Elsa and Harlan. 'Come on, you don't really believe them, do you?'

'It's real, Ryan,' Harlan replied sombrely. 'I promise you.'

Ryan crossed his arms. 'Prove it.'

Harlan removed the coin from his pocket and flipped it several metres above his head. It landed with a loud crack on the floorboards, balanced on its side.

Jes's mouth opened slowly. 'Whoa,' she murmured.

'That's only the start,' Harlan said. He looked at Ryan. 'Still don't believe me?'

Ryan shrugged, looking down at it. 'You made a coin land on its side. So what?'

'Has anyone seen Alyn?' Jes asked. 'I was hoping he might be here . . .'

Elsa looked at Harlan and quickly shook her head, remembering the sight of him with Blythe and Felix. 'No,' she said. 'Haven't seen him.'

While the group were talking, Charlie went into the main hall and found Luthan sorting through some plans of the opera house.

'You made it,' Luthan said, extending his hand. 'We hadn't heard from you. I was getting worried.'

Charlie pulled Luthan to one side. 'I didn't want to call in case our line was bugged, but there's been a problem,' he said. 'Henry's been taken prisoner.'

'Cool,' Elsa whispered with enthusiasm, lying on her mattress. It was the early hours of the morning and most of the others had gone to bed. 'I still can't believe you were shot . . .'

Jes smiled over from her bed. 'Don't know if cool's the right word, though,' she said, and pulled back her top to check the dressing, pressing gently with her fingers. 'But Ryan said he's jealous. Getting shot was on his list of things to do before he dies, apparently.'

'Most people want to swim with dolphins,' Elsa murmured, pulling a face. 'Do you remember much?'

Jes shook her head. 'It's a bit of a blur. I mean, I remember the sound more than anything. And Ryan's face . . . and I remember thinking of my mum and dad and wishing I could just . . .' She looked away.

'You don't want to talk about it,' Elsa said. 'That's fine. I get it. So what's the deal with this Henry guy?'

'You've got a lot of questions,' Jes said, smiling. She felt her eyes beginning to tire.

'Sorry,' Elsa mumbled. 'I'll shut up now, I promise.'

'It's fine.' Jes closed her eyes. 'The Guild knew something was going on with the prison. Henry was up there, investigating. He saved Ryan and me.'

'And?'

'He's in the prison . . .' she said, her voice trailing off. 'God knows what they'll do to him.'

'They'll try to get him to tell them about the Guild,' Elsa said, worrying. *If he talks, none of us will be safe here.*

She rolled over and tugged the blanket over her head.

A few hours had passed when Elsa became aware of a faint scratching sound. She sat up in bed and kept still. Moments later, she heard it again. *What was it? Where was it coming from?*

'Jes?' she whispered. 'Can you hear that?' But Jes was fast asleep. Elsa felt her heart begin to quicken.

She tiptoed out of bed and opened the door, looking out. The corridor was in darkness. *Maybe they have a pet cat or something*, Elsa thought, and was about to head back into bed when there was a loud thump from the locked room at the end of the corridor.

Elsa jumped with fright, shut the door and leapt back into her bed, pulling the covers over her face.

50

Julian caught the briefest reflection of his face in the computer monitor. Although he had always been slim, Julian now felt skinny, his body a mass of angles and protruding joints, and his eyes were tired and sunken.

'You almost finished?' said the manager of the deserted Internet cafe, looking at his watch. 'I need my lunch.'

'Just another couple of minutes,' Julian said, hammering at the keyboard.

'What are you doing anyway? You've been going at that for the past three hours. Last-minute homework or something?'

'Yes, that's exactly what I'm doing. Last-minute homework. *Idiot*,' Julian muttered. He logged off the computer and left.

He walked aimlessly for the next half an hour, rigid with cold. Each stab of wind struck his ears painfully, and he wiped a hand across his face, which felt numb and swollen.

The Guild's tower block wasn't far, and if he left now he could be there within an hour. But then he'd have to confront this 'Ability' they claimed that he had . . . and that meant he might've been responsible for his parents' death. The thought made him feel sick.

When he reached the end of the road Julian became aware of the slow rumble of a van behind him. He reached inside his coat for the ibis, struggling to move his stiff fingers round the trigger.

'Hey,' came a voice out of the van's window. Julian kept his eyes fixed directly ahead and walked quicker.

'Hey, kid,' the voice came again. 'You deaf or something?'

Julian looked over at the van just as the door flew open.

Pulling the ibis from his coat, Julian sprinted with it in his hand like a relay baton. *They must've been trailing me all this time.* He tore round the corner, barely keeping his balance on the ice, and ran down an alleyway, listening for the clatter of feet behind him.

At the next turning Julian spotted a large refuse container. He ducked behind it and waited.

'We lost him,' one of the men spat, less than a metre from where Julian was crouched, hidden. 'You two, try the next road.'

Julian watched the man's shadow extend a hand and pulled himself back to the wall. *He's going to see me,* he thought, looking around for an escape route. He clutched the ibis close to his chest.

The next thing he felt was a hand closing round his throat. He opened his eyes, faced with a smiling man.

'My employers have put quite a price on your head,' the man said.

'I'll p-pay you more,' Julian spluttered, trying to prise the hand away.

His attacker lowered his voice. 'You don't know who my employers are.'

Still flailing with the ibis in his other hand, Julian swung it as hard as he could at the man's head. His attacker stumbled back, releasing Julian momentarily.

Julian pushed past him and rushed out of the alleyway, sprinting as fast as he could along the street. When he was sure he was safe from danger, for now anyway, he looked back over his shoulder and released an explosive breath, panting so hard that his body shook. Right now, the Guild's offer didn't seem quite so bad.

Stephen stood at his office window, watching the swarm of pedestrians some way down on the street below. The winter sun poured mistily over the surrounding skyscrapers.

'Peasants,' he spat under his breath, as his lip rose into a sneer.

There was a knock at the door. 'Sir, I'm sorry to disturb you, but your website has been hacked. You might want to take a look.'

Stephen brought up his website on his computer. Across the front page were Julian's words:

YOU ARE A LIAR AND A CRIMINAL. YOU ARE NOT SAFE. I'M COMING FOR YOU.

Stephen shrieked. He knew straight away who was responsible: it was the escaped inmate, the boy who'd approached him in the crowd. He thought the words had been nothing more than an idle threat, but obviously the boy was more capable than he had imagined.

'Get this fixed immediately,' Stephen snarled through gritted teeth to his assistant, who immediately scurried away.

He dialled a number in his phone, and when it was answered promptly he said, 'It appears I have a deranged fan . . . I'm going to need extra security.'

51

'Well, well, here you are,' Luthan said, emerging on to the rooftop to find an eager Harlan waiting for him. 'No Elsa?'

Harlan shook his head. 'Haven't seen her around this morning.'

'A pity. She could use the practice.' Luthan clasped his hands behind his back. 'You requested an examination. Are you ready to proceed?'

'I'm ready,' Harlan said.

'Good. If you pass, you'll go on to the next level of training,' said Luthan. 'You'll learn things you never thought possible, Harlan.'

'I feel like my whole life has been leading to this,' Harlan said. 'I've never wanted anything more.'

'I can see you're determined,' Luthan went on. 'But are you ready to devote yourself to our cause?'

Harlan nodded. 'I am.'

'I must ask why. Why do you want to join the Guild? Is it *power* you desire? Or acceptance ... being part of something greater than yourself? Or is it because you want to help make the world a better place?'

Harlan thought about this for a moment and went to speak, but Luthan silenced him. 'I wasn't expecting you to answer just yet. But it's something for you to think about.'

Elsa peeked out from her hiding position behind the electricity generator. She looked down at the silver coin beside her foot. Still no luck. Sometimes she wondered whether she had the Ability at all.

'Before you begin,' continued Luthan, 'let me make it clear that we have rules for testing, Harlan – fail and you won't be able to retake the test for at least another month. Is that understood?'

'A month?' Harlan suddenly didn't feel so confident about his chances.

'We don't encourage time-wasting,' Luthan answered. 'But, remember, if you pass, another level of training awaits. So do you still want to take the test?'

Harlan removed the coin from his pocket and looked at it. 'Yeah. Let's do it.'

'You know what you have to do,' Luthan announced. 'Make it land on its edge . . . three times in a row. Good luck.'

Luthan stepped to the side and put his hands in his coat pockets.

Harlan flipped the coin, much higher than he'd intended on his first attempt, and watched as it returned to the ground, rolling on its side before falling still.

Nice one, Harlan, Elsa thought, restraining herself from cheering him on.

Harlan retrieved the coin and tossed it again, with more control this time. He swallowed and took a deep breath as the coin landed directly on its side, wobbling a little.

'That's twice,' said Luthan. 'Once more, Harlan. Remember to concentrate . . .'

Harlan nodded. He positioned the coin on his thumb, then closed his eyes and flipped it, waiting for the satisfying clink of metal on stone. Elsa shut her eyes, fearing that he was going to fail. The coin landed, rolled to a halt, wobbled ever so slightly and toppled over.

Elsa opened her eyes. She looked at the coin, then at a clearly devastated Harlan.

'I'm sorry,' Luthan said. 'It didn't land on its side. I can't allow you to pass.' He offered a consoling smile and walked past the boy to the stairs.

Harlan ran over to the coin in disbelief. 'Wait!' he said, calling after Luthan. 'That's it? Don't I at least get another try?'

'I told you the rules. I'll see you in a month's time. Keep practising, Harlan.'

Before Harlan could say another word, Luthan disappeared.

Elsa hopped out from behind the electricity generator. 'Hey, I'm sorry you didn't pass, Harlan,' she said. 'You were doing really well. I'd have passed you –'

'*You*,' Harlan said. 'That's why it didn't work. It was you being here –'

Elsa pointed to herself innocently. 'Me? What have I done? I just came to cheer you on, is all –'

'And *you* jinxed it.' Harlan scowled at her. 'It was going to work, but you cancelled it out. Now I have to wait and you'll probably pass before I do!'

Elsa looked hurt. 'Well, I'm sorry for coming. I wish I'd never bothered.' With that, she turned and ran away.

52

It was long past noon when Ryan eventually awoke. He stumbled groggily from his bed and went into the meeting room.

Jes and Elsa were sitting round a table with Anton, who was teaching a delighted Elsa a card trick.

'Look at this, Ryan!' she exclaimed, thrusting a fanned deck of cards in his face. 'Choose one. Go on . . .'

'Don't like magic tricks,' he grumbled. 'They're stupid.' He sat in the chair next to Jes, rubbing his eyes. 'So what are we gonna do?'

'We're going to kidnap one of the Pledge at the opera house and use them to stop the project,' said Elsa.

'*You* aren't doing anything,' Anton answered. '*We* are.'

'Hang on a minute,' Ryan cut in. '*We*'re the ones they put in that place. And you're telling me we can't do this ourselves? We don't need you lot.'

'Of course we need them,' Harlan argued, entering the room. He scowled at Elsa.

'You're forgetting that we've saved your skin repeatedly,' said Anton, looking at Ryan.

'We broke out of the prison without any of you,' Ryan snapped.

Anton could see Ryan was quickly becoming irritated. 'You got lucky,' he said, shrugging.

'I don't even want to join your gang or whatever you are!' Ryan said, and got to his feet. 'I don't believe in any of this stuff. It's crazy. Come with me, Jes. You too, Elsa.' He looked at Harlan. 'And you too, if you want . . .'

'I'm not going anywhere.' Harlan shook his head slowly. 'I'm staying here. This is the best thing that's ever happened to me. I want to be a part of this.'

Ryan rolled his eyes and turned to Elsa and Jes. 'What about you two?'

'I'm pretty rubbish at it, but I'm with Harlan,' Elsa said, and smiled consolingly. 'This is pretty cool.'

'Jes?'

Jes thought about it for a moment and sighed.

'Come on, Jes,' Ryan said. 'You can't be serious . . .'

'I'm not going to put my family at risk by going back home, Ryan,' she said.

'So you're going to stay with this lot?' He looked up as Pyra entered the room. She was wearing a white T-shirt and grey jogging bottoms. 'And who are you?'

'We haven't yet been introduced,' she said. 'Come with me, Ryan. And anyone else who wants to join in.'

He looked suspicious. 'Why? Where are we going?'

'We're going to do some training,' she said.

'I've heard about your training. Flipping a coin again and again and again until it drives you nuts,' Ryan challenged. 'I've got better things to do with my time – no offence, Harlan.'

'No coins,' Pyra said. 'I mean martial arts. You want to learn how to fight, Ryan?'

'I can fight already. I was the toughest in my school.'

Pyra shoved Ryan hard. He fell back into the chair. 'What's the big idea?'

He got up and went to shove Pyra back, but she grabbed him and effortlessly flipped him off his feet. He landed with a thud, much to the amusement of the others.

'Ha! The look on your face,' Elsa said, pointing at him and grinning.

Ryan swatted her hand away and hopped back up. 'You caught me off guard,' he grumbled. 'You'd never get me if I was –'

Before he could finish speaking, Pyra darted to the side, hoisted him across her shoulders and gently released him on to the floor.

Ryan expelled a gust of air from his mouth. 'What are you playing at?' he panted, a little winded, and swiped at her feet. 'Trying to embarrass me in front of everyone?'

He caught Jes's eyes and blushed a little, then made another grab for Pyra's feet. She hopped away gracefully.

'I think you should accept her offer,' said Jes. 'Looks like you need the training . . .'

Pyra reached down and helped Ryan get to his feet. 'Once you understand how the Ability works, you can use it in all areas where there is some degree of chance . . . like influencing people . . . like *fighting* . . .'

Ryan shifted his weight and scratched the back of his neck.

'It gives you an edge. An advantage. And that's exactly what you're going to need, until the Pledge is defeated.' She looked at the others. 'Anyone else coming?'

'As much as I'd like to beat Ryan up, I can't just yet.' Jes smiled, patting her side.

'Looks like it's just you and me, Ryan,' Pyra announced.

53

Alyn and Felix were sitting in silence in the kitchen in Felix's penthouse. Although it was only a little after noon, the sunlight was struggling to pierce the heavy grey clouds. Alyn's tailor-made tuxedo had just been delivered and was hanging from the door.

'Stephen will react badly when we tell him he's expelled from the Pledge,' said Felix, the first thing he had said in some time. 'But alone he is no match for the rest of us. And that's not even including Emmanuel . . .'

Alyn looked baffled. 'Emmanuel? You didn't tell me there was another member.'

'I haven't introduced you yet. Emmanuel is my adviser. It was his suggestion all along that we start the project.'

This was enough to quieten Alyn, who until that point was convinced Felix was the mastermind behind it all.

'They did a good job with the tuxedo, don't you think?' Felix said, changing the subject.

'Look, Felix, you got me mixed up in all of this,' Alyn

said. 'If you want me to help you, I need to know everyone who's involved. Everyone.'

Felix pulled himself out of the chair. 'Emmanuel and I are due to meet. Soon. Perhaps you'd like to join us.'

'All right. When?'

'I don't know,' Felix said. 'Whenever he decides to show himself.'

Alyn frowned. 'I thought you were leader of this whole thing.'

'I'm the wealthiest man in the country,' Felix announced sternly. 'And I'm the leader of the Pledge. I hold *reality* in my fingertips. *Me*. Not Stephen, not Emmanuel. I'm the one in charge, Alyn.'

With a sigh Alyn got to his feet and walked over to the dining table. Hanging from the back of one of the chairs was a red demonic-looking mask. Alyn slipped the mask on and stared through the window, past his own face to the reflection of the chandelier. He focused intently on the almond-shaped lights in turn, until each one went out.

'Did you do that?' asked Felix.

'Yeah,' Alyn said, staring again at the city below. 'I did.'

'You blew each light bulb in a row,' Felix said. 'Remarkable. It would normally take a room full of you to do that, and there's no telling when it might happen. This was . . . instantaneous.'

Alyn removed the mask and tossed it on to the table, a satisfied smile across his lips.

He walked past Felix, who was examining the chandelier with his fingertips. 'You've got an exciting future ahead of you, Alyn,' Felix said.

54

'What's the best thing to do when you're confronted, Ryan?' asked Pyra.

Ryan had changed into a black hooded jumper for his training session. The pair were stood together in a deserted playground a hundred or so metres from the tower block, surrounded by scattering leaves.

Ryan shrugged. 'Depends how big they are, I suppose. If they're this big,' he said, measuring with his hands, 'then a headbutt should do it. Any taller than that and I'd probably just kick 'em in the –'

Pyra gestured for him to stop. 'The best thing to do when you're confronted is to run away, not fight. Fighting's always a last resort. I mean, you really think Harlan and Julian could've fought their way past that gang?'

'Harlan and Julian?' He grinned. 'Ha, not likely . . .'

'You know what I mean. It could've easily been you and Jes there. Or you and Elsa. You ever heard of parkour?'

'You mean, like, jumping over stuff?'

Pyra nodded. 'The art of escape,' she said.

She took several steps back and ran at the metal railing. Placing one hand gently on it, she sailed over effortlessly and used the momentum to sprint towards a brick wall. She leapt at the wall, using her feet to push herself up, and then pulled herself to the top. She walked a few steps along the narrow edge, turned and back-flipped. Ryan had watched the whole thing in awe, and with a sinking feeling in his stomach.

'If you use the Ability, you'll find it a lot easier,' she said. 'You'll be able to make jumps and landings you probably wouldn't be able to otherwise.' She walked back over and stood beside Ryan. 'Start with jumping that railing.'

Ryan lowered himself. He looked at Pyra, who nodded permission. After a deep breath, Ryan charged at the railing, yelling what sounded like a battle cry. As he neared it, he slowed, positioned his hands cautiously, and attempted to vault. Almost immediately he folded, his legs tangled together and he landed crumpled across the horizontal beam. He hung there, suspended for a few painful seconds, before slowly unrolling and landing on his back.

Before Pyra could say anything, Ryan was back on his feet and speeding at it a second time. Again, his feet caught and he tripped mid-air, slamming against the rubber playground surface with a dull slap.

'Hey, I appreciate that you're giving it another go, but –'

Ryan was up again, red-faced and yelling at the railing. He threw himself up at it, this time misplacing his hands and tying himself in a knot.

Once more he landed on his back, panting, and was a lot slower getting to his feet.

'Ryan, you'll be black and blue at this rate. They'll think I beat the crap out of you. You have to really want to do it. You need to see it in your mind and convince the world and all its elements around you that you are going to make it.'

'I can do it,' he wheezed. He limped into a starting position, leaning into his knees. 'I won't let it win.'

He sprinted at the metal railing, this time in silence, his arms chopping at his sides. As he neared it, Ryan outstretched his hand and vaulted. He could see his legs rise up out of the corner of his eye. *I'm doing it*, he thought. *I'm over . . .*

He hit the ground with a jolt and let the momentum carry him a few extra metres.

'Good,' Pyra said, clapping.

'Yeah!' he agreed, trying to reclaim his breath. 'It was pretty good, wasn't it?' *Maybe this thing isn't so bad after all.*

He wiped his forehead with the sleeve of his jumper. 'You said something before about the Ability. About it being good for fighting . . .'

'And running away . . .'

'And changing someone's mind?' Ryan asked. 'That's what I want to learn next. When will you show me that?'

'Manipulating people is something we try to avoid,' said Pyra. 'There are a lot of ethical problems.'

'Sure. But you would show me at some point, right?'

'Once you pass the basic training, maybe,' Pyra said. 'Whose mind are you trying to change anyway?'

'Oh, no one's,' he said.

'Go on – tell me, Ryan.'

He shrugged. 'Just this girl,' he said. 'I used to fancy her a bit . . .'

Pyra frowned. 'You're trying to get her to like you?'

Ryan looked down. 'Nah. Not really. I mean, I was just wondering.'

'Jes,' said Pyra. 'That's who you're talking about, isn't it?'

Ryan felt himself going red. He shook his head.

'I could have you kicked out for saying something like that,' Pyra said, struggling to control her anger.

'Eh? Why are you getting so uptight about it?' he said. 'It's not like I even believe all this rubbish anyway.'

Pyra glared at him and walked away. 'You can find someone else to train you.'

The Guild had been discussing their plans in private for the past hour. A curious Elsa was loitering outside in the hall, pressing her ear against the oak doors. It was no good; she couldn't hear a thing. She skipped round to the adjoining corridor and paused in front of the locked door at the end.

Had she really heard something coming from there last night? After all, it had been late and buildings made all kinds of creaks and groans in the night as they got cooler and contracted. That's what her parents told her anyway. Then again, she'd woken them so many times with claims that she'd heard ghosts – and monsters – in her bedroom that they'd probably have told her anything to keep her quiet.

And what she'd heard last night hadn't sounded like anything she'd heard before.

As she was standing there, in silence, Elsa thought she heard something. A soft scraping sound. It sounded like it came from behind the door, she thought.

She paused, then slowly brought herself level with the keyhole. 'Hey, is someone in there?' she whispered and immediately her pulse quickened.

Nothing. She moved closer still, pressing both hands to the door.

Again, a scrape, a shuffle. More distinct this time. Then another sound: a tap.

She got down to her knees and tried to peer underneath.

'I thought you were told not to come here,' said Luthan, from behind her.

Elsa gasped. 'Oh, I'm sorry, I just – I thought I heard something.'

'It was probably the floorboards.' He put a hand on her shoulder and steered her away. 'You're under our care, which means you live by our rules. Understood?'

Elsa nodded, looking back at the door a final time.

'So have you been practising with the coin? Do you think you might be ready to take your test soon?'

Elsa shook her head. 'If Harlan can't do it, I've got no chance.'

Luthan smiled and gestured to her and Jes's room. 'Your friends are all in there. Please try not to wander.'

'Are you OK, Elsa? You look confused,' said Jes, as Elsa came in.

'I'm fine,' she said, still thinking about her peculiar encounter with Luthan. 'So what have I missed?'

'Our favourite person,' said Harlan, who was gazing out of the window. 'Look.'

Elsa pushed past him and leant out. Below them, walking quickly across the frost-covered grass towards the tower block, was Julian.

'*Julian!*' Elsa shouted out of the window, waving to him.

The Guild member on guard duty approached Julian threateningly.

'It's all right!' Elsa yelled down, cupping her hand round her mouth. 'He's one of us!'

'I wonder what he's after,' Jes said. 'Does this mean we have to watch our backs?'

'Knowing Julian, he's probably on the Pledge's side by now anyway,' Ryan remarked, cocking an eyebrow.

'No big welcome then?' Julian declared, extending his arms from his sides, as he was escorted to the boys' bedroom.

'We weren't sure you were even coming back,' Harlan said.

'Changed my mind. I've come to make you an offer,' he said. 'I'm going after the Pledge.'

'For what? Revenge?'

Julian smiled. 'Is there anything more noble? Besides, I've had a few run-ins with a certain young billionaire, and I've taken great offence to him thinking he can outwit me . . .'

'Yeah, well, you're too late.' Ryan sighed, folding his arms. 'This bunch are already on it.'

'The Pledge will be at some stupid opera thing tomorrow night,' Elsa explained. 'But the Guild is already planning to attack and take a hostage!'

'And we aren't allowed to join in,' Ryan grumbled, flopping his head back on the pillow of his bed.

Julian wandered to the window. He breathed on the glass and made a squiggle shape with his finger. 'The opera house it is,' he said slowly. 'I say we join them.'

'And do what?' Harlan said. 'We'll be walking into the lion's den. We don't even have a plan . . .'

'There'll be a room full of powerful and influential people,' Julian said. 'There'll be cameras. And, let's not forget, all of *us* are technically missing. What better time or place to tell them our story? And there's no way the Pledge will send their thugs after us – not in front of everyone.'

'We'll be getting in the Guild's way,' Elsa declared.

'Or they'll be getting in ours,' Julian answered. 'Time's running out. Who's with me?'

He waited until the group had each raised their hands before giving a thin smile. 'Then we go,' he said. 'Tomorrow night.'

55

It was soon Friday afternoon. After a morning of practising the Ability under the watchful eyes of Guild members, the group at last had the chance to assemble in Jes and Elsa's bedroom for a secret meeting. They sat in a circle on the floor, while Julian gazed out of the window, his agile eyes darting back and forth in deep concentration.

'This thing starts at six,' Ryan said, 'so we'll need to leave as soon as we can to get there before everyone arrives. Trouble is, how are we gonna get in? There'll be bouncers.'

Elsa looked at Harlan. 'Can't you use the Ability to make them let us in?'

'You mean manipulation?' Harlan shook his head. 'That's too advanced. I only know the basics, like affecting gravity.'

Julian snorted. 'Put too much faith in that stuff and you stop using *this*,' he said, tapping the side of his head. 'There's a back entrance down a side alley. If we get there early enough, the door should be unlocked for staff. What to do when we're inside is another matter.'

'We just need to get to the stage,' Jes said. 'We can announce it as soon as the performance is finished. I bet there'll be some cameras. We'll run on and tell the entire crowd what's happened. It'll be on the Internet in no time.'

'But they'll have plenty of security,' Ryan said. 'They'll drag us off before we can say a thing and then we'll have given ourselves to the Pledge.'

'But we've got ibises!' Elsa exclaimed. 'A couple of us can hold them off until we get our story out, right?'

'Count me in,' Ryan said. 'Never was one for speeches. But what can we say? What'll make them listen?'

'We tell them our names and when we went missing,' Harlan said. 'We tell them about the others in the prison. It'll be all over the news. Our parents will see us . . .'

He looked at Elsa, whose eyes lit up at hearing this. She imagined the headline: TEENAGERS HIJACK OPERA. But when the media understood they had all been missing for several months, she was sure *someone* would sit up and listen. It would only take one interested party to check the forest and they'd find the prison soon enough.

'They'll realize we were telling the truth,' she said, beaming. 'They'll lock up the Pledge and throw away the key . . . and we'll be safe!' She looked out of the window at the patrolling guard below. 'Guess they thought we'd try to leave. Now we just have to find a way past him.'

'I have an idea,' Jes said, gathering the sheets from the beds. 'Come with me.'

*

234

The group stealthily made their way down the winding stairwell to the second floor, avoiding the Guild members who were busy with their own preparation for the event. Jes crept along to the nearest door and turned the handle. It opened into a vast, empty open-plan room with dusty wooden floors. Jes beckoned them over to the wall of windows at the rear of the building and peered outside. From this floor, the drop was only about five metres to the grass below.

Jes tied a bedsheet round a pipe next to the window and tugged to make sure it was secure. She took another sheet and fastened both together with a firm knot.

'Wait,' Ryan urged, as Jes was reaching out of the window. The Guild's sentry was ambling slowly past, looking back and forth.

'Now,' he urged, once the man had disappeared round the corner.

Jes dropped the bedsheet rope out of the window and turned to Julian. 'Go on.'

'I'm not going first . . .' He backed away and gestured for Elsa to go before him.

'Why is it always me?' Elsa huffed under her breath. 'Does this bedsheet thing even work in real life?' she asked.

'We're about to find out,' Julian said with an encouraging shove.

Fortunately for the group, it did, and minutes later all five were free from the tower block, hurrying to the nearest tube station.

56

'Opera isn't really my thing, Alyn,' Felix said, adjusting the mask, a white half-moon shape that sat a little clumsily across his face. 'This masquerade party is quite enough, let alone having someone warbling at me for hours.'

Alyn fiddled with his tuxedo. 'When are we done?' he said, before clarifying. 'Our agreement, I mean.'

'Tonight,' Felix said. 'As soon as Stephen's expulsion from the Pledge is announced.'

Alyn turned to him. 'And you'll free everyone, like you promised?'

Felix was silent for a moment. 'Yes,' he said.

You'd better, Alyn thought, studying him closely.

'Our car has arrived,' Felix said. 'Go and tell him I'll be another five minutes. I'll meet you down there.'

Alyn took the lift to the ground floor. He left the foyer, pushed open the glass doors and jogged down the steps. The black limousine was parked at the kerb.

Alyn tapped on the driver's window. 'Mr Felix sends his apologies. He'll be a few more minutes.'

'Not a problem,' said the driver. 'Jump in the back.'

Alyn went to the rear of the car and through the window he could just make out the shape of a lone figure. The window lowered and a man with neat black hair and intensely focused eyes looked up at Alyn. He wore a sharp grey suit, the colour of which reminded Alyn of his own prison uniform.

'Oh, hello. I'm Alyn, Mr Felix's ... assistant,' Alyn said, extending his hand politely.

The stranger watched Alyn's hand until it withdrew. 'How interesting. My name is Emmanuel. I'm his adviser. Come, sit with me.'

Alyn obediently opened the door and slid in. He smiled nervously as Emmanuel studied him, almost imperceptibly sniffing the air.

'Felix's apprentice,' Emmanuel pondered. 'Of all people, I wonder why he chose you ...'

'I impressed Mr Felix during the interview,' Alyn said defensively. *I don't trust this guy one bit*, he thought. There seemed to be a peculiar, sinister force seeping from him, and Alyn felt the skin on the back of his neck prickle.

'You and I both know that's a lie,' Emmanuel answered coolly. 'I can sense you have a great power, Alyn.'

'I – I don't know what you're talking about. Anyway, I need to speak with Mr Felix,' Alyn said, avoiding the subject. A little flustered, he pulled the handle and the door swung open. He stood just in time to see Felix coming towards him in a black tuxedo, a white scarf draped across his shoulders. Alyn looked back at the car anxiously. The door was now closed.

'Is something wrong?' Felix asked. 'You look like something's bothering you.'

'Mr Felix, I just spoke with your adviser,' Alyn whispered, pulling him to one side. 'Something's not right about him.'

'My adviser,' Felix said, pushing past him. 'You mean Emmanuel?'

'Yeah,' Alyn hissed. He made eyes at Felix. 'He's in there now. I don't trust him . . .'

Felix looked at Alyn with some concern and opened the door to peer inside. 'There's no one in here, Alyn,' he said. 'The car is just for us.'

'What?'

Felix stepped out of the way so Alyn could see inside.

Alyn stepped away from the car, shaking his head slowly. He went up to the chauffeur's window.

'That man who was in the car just now,' he said, becoming more panicked by the second. 'Where is he? Where did he go?'

'There was no one else in here,' the chauffeur said blankly.

'He was sitting in the back just now!'

'I'm afraid I don't know about that, young man . . .'

Felix placed a hand on Alyn's shoulder and looked at his watch. 'Forget it, Alyn. We have to get moving.' He held the door open and gestured for a speechless Alyn to climb inside, then followed after him.

*

Pyra, Anton and Luthan drove through the streaming rain in the silver sports car, followed by a second car. Rather than her usual leather jacket and torn jeans, Pyra was wearing a black strapless dress, a three-quarter-length designer coat and heels. Luthan wore a tuxedo with a silk cummerbund round his waist.

'The pair of you look pretty convincing,' Anton said as he parked down a quiet street a short way from the opera house.

'This needs to be seamless,' Luthan said, pushing open his door. 'We've got half an hour after the opera finishes before this masquerade starts. There'll be a drinks reception. This is when I'll influence Felix to leave.'

'I'll make sure the others are distracted,' Pyra said. 'I'll meet up with you in the hall. We knock Felix out and carry him outside, pretending he's had too much to drink.'

Anton nodded. 'Where I'll be waiting.' He adjusted his flat cap in the mirror and watched the second car parking at the end of the street. 'There's our back-up, if anything goes wrong.'

'Right, we're on,' Luthan said, looking at Pyra. He stepped out of the car and crooked his arm for Pyra to take. She grabbed it and the pair walked towards the front entrance of the opera house.

'I'm sorry,' said the doorman at the top of the marble steps, quickly moving in front of them to block their entry. 'There's a performance starting shortly and we have a charity ball afterwards . . .'

'We know,' said Pyra with a faux sweetness. 'That's why we're here.'

'It's a VIP event,' the doorman said smugly. 'I need to see your invitation or I can't let you in.'

'You recognize us surely?' Luthan said, and gestured to both himself and Pyra.

'I don't know either of you,' he said, looking blank.

'We came in earlier,' Luthan argued. 'You must have forgotten. A simple mistake.'

The doorman looked at them both, a little incredulous, and said, 'If you don't leave, I'll have to call security.'

For the past minute or so Pyra had been twirling the domino between her fingers. A single rogue molecule within one of the doorman's neurons caused it to generate an action potential, triggering a minor chain reaction of crackling synapses. Amid the chemical fireworks in his brain a phantom memory formed.

'You don't really want to embarrass yourself by calling security,' Pyra said.

'No, of course not. I'm sorry,' he said, having some vague notion that he'd seen the pair arrive already.

Pyra and Luthan stepped inside. The interior of the opera house seemed to glow with gold and ochre, lights reflecting from every polished surface.

'Down here,' Luthan said to Pyra, leading her towards a crowded corridor. 'We need to mingle until it starts.'

They walked quickly, footsteps clacking on the smooth marble.

*

'This is it,' Julian said, as the group turned in to the alleyway.

Despite their plans to get to the opera house as soon as possible, the group had got completely lost and managed to lose Elsa twice in the space of an hour. Now running behind schedule and anxious with anticipation, a collective silence had fallen upon them.

The cobblestones glistened under the hazy glow pouring from the streetlight.

'That supposed to be our way in?' Ryan asked, nodding to a small metal door. He walked over and gave it a shove. 'It's locked. Damn it! We're too late.' He stepped back a few paces and launched a kick at it.

'Ryan, you moron! Someone might hear you from the other side,' Elsa said, pulling him away.

'I've spotted another way in,' Julian muttered, looking at a small square window open some way above them.

'All the way up there?' Jes said. 'Good luck, Julian.'

'If one of us gets in, they can open the door from inside,' Julian answered. 'Someone give me a boost up . . .'

Harlan knelt beneath the window and cupped his hands. Julian stepped on and tried grasping for the window.

'I still can't reach it,' he spat, rain pouring into his eyes.

'Out of the way,' Ryan said, moving back several metres. He handed Jes his ibis, then sped at the wall and jumped, aiming with the ball of his foot. As he gained momentum, he reached up with his fingertips, missing the window by centimetres, then landed back on the ground.

'That Pyra or whatever her name is showed me it,' he said, calming himself with a deep breath. 'Let me try again.'

He ran at the wall again, bounced up and made a desperate grab for the narrow sill of the window.

'This isn't going to work,' Julian said. 'We'll end up alerting security –'

'You aren't helping by thinking like that,' Harlan cut in. 'You'll end up jinxing him.'

Elsa nodded, blushing a little as she remembered how she'd caused Harlan's coin test to fail.

'Harlan's right. If we all focus on it, it should help, right? Go on, Ryan, I think you can do it!'

Ryan walked back further and lowered down again, imagining himself gripping the window ledge.

'You can do it, Ryan,' Harlan said. He shut his eyes, visualizing Ryan's success.

Ryan charged at the wall and bounced, this time gaining enough momentum and traction from the wall to carry him up towards the window. There was a sudden tingling sensation in his mind as he threw his arms up, just reaching the ledge with his fingertips. He hung there suspended for a moment while the others watched below. 'I'm there!' he spluttered, amazed that he had managed it.

He grunted and hoisted himself through the window until all that remained in view were his dangling legs.

*

In the back of the car Stephen sat with the fox mask on the seat next to him. He held an ibis in his hands, twirling it back and forth. Since the attack on his website Stephen hadn't travelled anywhere without a van of thugs following for protection.

'Stop here,' he ordered the driver.

The driver pulled the limousine up to the pavement. A tired-looking homeless man was sat in the doorway of a closed shop with a tattered cap in front of him. Inside were a couple of coins.

'You there,' Stephen shouted out of the window. He clicked his fingers.

The homeless man pointed at himself.

'Yes,' said Stephen. 'Come on, I haven't got all day.'

The man creaked to his feet, gathering his cap close to his chest. He tottered towards the car and leant inside.

Stephen removed a wad of money from his pocket. The man's eyes widened.

'Have you ever seen this much money in your life?' Stephen asked.

The man, mesmerized by the fan of notes, shook his head. 'No, sir.'

'Daddy used to give me this much pocket money every week as soon I was old enough to walk!' Stephen released a delighted shriek and fanned the money at the other man. 'I'll give it to you. But first I want you to do something for me.'

'Anything,' the man said. 'I'll do anything you want, sir.'

A cruel smile slid across Stephen's lips. 'Pretend that you're a dog.'

'A dog?'

'Yes,' Stephen said, smirking. 'Here. On the pavement.'

The man considered this for barely a second, then dropped to his knees and began howling.

Hysterical, Stephen started clapping. 'More!' he cried. 'Louder!'

The man crawled on all fours towards a couple of pedestrians, barking at them. They quickly hurried past.

Stephen was laughing so much that his cheeks were pink and a single curl of hair had become displaced from his immaculately combed side parting.

The man finished barking, erupting into a coughing fit, and crawled on damp knees towards the car window. 'Sir,' he said, 'am I finished now?'

Stephen picked up the fox mask from the seat and put it on. 'Go away, little dog,' Stephen said from behind the mask. 'I don't want to play any more.'

The homeless man got to his feet and lunged towards the money.

Stephen pointed the ibis through the window and fired. The man fell some way back, landing in a puddle. Stephen reached out of the window and released the money from his fingertips. Most of the notes slipped down the drain by the kerb, sailing on the rainwater, while the few remaining ones scattered in the wind and rain.

Stephen's fit of laughter was disrupted by his

mobile phone ringing. 'You're interrupting something important, so this better be good, or I'll –'

'Check the news,' Susannah said.

Stephen turned on the television screen embedded in the back seat and jabbed it until he found a twenty-four-hour news channel.

'I'm waiting . . .' he said impatiently.

'Now,' Susannah said on the other end of the line.

Stephen gasped, stroking the leather seat with his soft white hands as the screen changed to a picture of Felix's company logo and an accompanying headline. 'Oh, this is just wonderful, Ms Dion. *Just wonderful!*'

He nodded to the driver to go and the black limousine pulled away from the kerb and towards the opera house.

57

Ryan fell through the window and landed in a large trolley filled with bundles of coloured fabric. He crept out, checking that nobody was around, and opened the door, letting the others inside.

'Now we just gotta find a way down to the stage,' he said, looking left and right along the corridor.

The group was halted suddenly by approaching footsteps.

'In here,' Jes said, and pulled Harlan into a cleaning cupboard. Julian, Ryan and Elsa all leapt into the trolley and pulled the fabric across them.

'This lot is to go down to the stage,' they heard a voice say. 'Try to get a move on, we're running late.'

'Yes, sir,' said another voice. The man took hold of the trolley handles and with some considerable effort managed to get it moving.

The trolley rolled and rattled down the length of the corridor.

'We've lost Jes and Harlan!' Elsa whispered. 'We'll have to go back for them.'

'We're not going anywhere, they'll catch up with us,' Julian replied quietly. 'This'll take us exactly where we need to be.'

The trolley was wheeled behind the stage. The trio waited for the busy stage hands to pass before they climbed out and peered at the mostly empty auditorium. The walls were decorated with shells, shapes and carved flowers, which glinted through the shadows like coral.

'Do you have your ibis?' Elsa whispered to Ryan. They paused as a group of chattering assistants emerged and walked right past them, completely oblivious to the three intruders.

'Nah. Gave it to Jes to hold. Guess that screws up our plan. Anyway, we need somewhere to hide,' he said, searching for a suitable spot. He hopped on to the stage and noticed some wires coming from below. 'Look, we can go under and wait for the right moment,' he said.

Before they had a chance, though, a tall stressed-looking man in a suit and glasses came marching towards them. He gestured with a rolled-up piece of paper, waving it like a baton. 'There you are, our missing extras! We've been looking everywhere for you!'

'Extras?' said a baffled Elsa. 'But we aren't –'

'The director was taken ill earlier, so I'm in charge of you now. What are the three of you playing at? The performance starts in less than half an hour!'

Julian, Ryan and Elsa all looked at one another. 'We're sorry,' Julian said, improvising. 'We were just looking for our costumes . . .'

The man gave them a contemptuous glare. He stomped towards the trolley, reached inside and removed three threadbare school uniforms, covered in patches. 'Put your costumes on and get yourselves ready.'

Each of the three reluctantly took a uniform and was shoved behind the stage.

'No way,' Ryan hissed, after putting on his costume. His shorts were several sizes too small and the tatty patchwork top barely fit round his broad chest. 'I'm not doing it. I'm not going on.'

Julian appeared beside him, wearing a similar pair of shorts, socks hitched to his knees and a child's school cap balanced precariously on top of his head. Elsa erupted in a fit of laughter at seeing the pair. She clutched her stomach.

Julian glared at her. 'I'm glad you find it so funny. At least no one else is around to see this fiasco.' Barely a moment after the words left his lips, one of the stagehands appeared, with a camera poised in their direction.

'You dare,' Ryan threatened, but not before a flash blinked. Ryan ran towards him and knocked the camera out of his hands.

'What are you doing?' the young man cried, reaching down to salvage the camera. 'Don't you guys want a picture?'

'No,' Ryan growled.

'*No*,' Julian agreed. 'No pictures.' He pushed past the crouched man. 'Let's just get this over and done with.'

*

'The trolley went down that corridor,' Jes said, opening the cupboard door. Harlan slipped out and the pair followed the winding passage, leading them through an ornate maze of beige and gold.

Jes peered through a door at the end to find a room filled with fluttering young actors.

'Back up,' she said to Harlan. 'We can't go in there.' Holding his ibis inside his coat sleeve, Harlan scurried up a staircase that led off the corridor. He paused to wait for her at the top.

Jes pulled herself up the stairs using the banister, and clutched her side.

'This way is clear,' Harlan said, treading lightly across the plush red carpeting.

They dived into the nearest room. Running the length of an enormous wall were three rectangular tables lined with champagne glasses and silver ice buckets.

Two waiters, a boy and a girl wearing black shirts, were drizzling champagne into the slim glasses. They both looked up at Jes and Harlan.

'Who are you?' the boy said. 'This is a private area.'

'We're here to help,' Harlan lied. 'We're . . . we're the new staff.'

'New staff? I don't know anything about this. Have you both had security checks?' the girl said. 'There are some very important people due here shortly.'

'We know,' said Jes.

'Let me see your passes,' said the girl.

'Er, we forgot them?' Jes claimed unsuccessfully.

The girl lowered the black and gold bottle of champagne she was holding and marched over to the wall telephone. 'You're not supposed to be up here,' she said. 'I'm calling security.'

As soon as she had removed the telephone, Harlan pulled the ibis out of his pocket and fired. The girl hit the wall and collapsed to the ground. Her colleague raised his trembling hands in defeat, but Harlan sent him horizontal with another ibis blast.

'Sorry,' he said to the pair, then turned to Jes. 'We need somewhere to put them.'

Jes looked around and noticed a velvety maroon drape. She pulled it aside, revealing a cupboard door; inside was a mop, a couple of rolls of kitchen paper and some spare black shirts hanging from a hook. She yanked the shirts off the hook and threw them out.

'In here!' she said. Harlan lifted the boy into the cupboard, pushing his arms inside with his foot. They both picked up the girl and positioned her inside, beside the boy. With relief they closed the door behind them and pulled the drape back to conceal it.

'We should make the most of these uniforms – if anyone asks, we can say we're the waiting staff,' he said, pulling off his coat and T-shirt. He looked at Jes, who was standing awkwardly with her coat in her hands. He flashed her an embarrassed smile and looked away. 'Then we can head down to the stage to find the others.'

Jes quickly removed her jumper and frantically pulled on the black shirt.

At that moment, the door opened and in stepped an overweight man in a tuxedo. Patches of sweat blotted his white shirt. He dabbed at his face with a handkerchief. 'Some of the guests have already started to arrive,' he announced. 'I don't need to remind you how important they are.'

'Yes, sir,' Jes and Harlan agreed in cautious unison.

'Good grief, whatever is wrong with you?' the man said. He marched over to Jes and pointed at the buttons of her shirt. 'You look a wreck, girl! Shirt ill-fitting and untucked ... and jeans! You were told to wear black trousers!'

'Sorry, sir,' said Jes.

He looked at Harlan. 'And you're just as bad. Get yourselves looking presentable at once. And where are your masks?'

Jes looked around and spotted two masks, one black, one white, on the table. 'Here,' she said, and passed one to Harlan, placing hers over her face.

'That's more like it. Now try to show a little enthusiasm, or I'll find another pair who can.' With that, the man pivoted on his polished heel and stomped away.

'That was close,' said Harlan with a grin, hiding the ibis. Outside, the sound of several hundred pairs of feet filled the corridor.

58

Downstairs, Pyra and Luthan watched carefully as a deluge of tuxedoed guests arrived in the grand entrance hall, a sauntering swarm of silk and sequins.

'There's Stephen,' she whispered, averting her gaze as he slithered past.

'And Blythe.' Luthan gestured with his eyes. Pyra looked over her shoulder as the red-faced, moustached aristocrat stomped into the hall, almost knocking a delicate-looking white-haired woman off her feet.

'He looks drunk already,' Pyra said, pulling a face.

'He probably is. Where the hell is Felix?'

She checked anxiously over Luthan's shoulder.

A sprightly man with aquiline features hopped on to the staircase and drummed lightly at a wine glass with a spoon until the conversation in the hall fell silent.

'Ladies and gentlemen, I'm honoured that you could be here tonight to attend this very special performance, which will be commencing shortly. And afterwards, as you know, we will retire to the ballroom for a masquerade party.' He stopped and clasped his hands by his navel. 'I want to offer my most gracious thanks to young Stephen Nover for all his kind contributions to this event. A round of applause, I think, is in order.'

The room rippled with applause, as a grinning Stephen bowed.

Pyra folded her arms, refusing to clap.

'Don't make it too obvious,' Luthan whispered, tapping his hands gently.

Their host swept his hand to the side and gestured for the attendees to ascend the staircase. Pyra and Luthan followed the heaving crowd to the VIP room.

'Champagne?' Harlan said from behind his white mask. He extended a glass to a blonde lady wearing a fur coat.

'Ask her if she would "like some champagne",' the overweight event organizer spat in Harlan's ear. 'My goodness, wherever did they find you?'

Harlan looked over at a flustered Jes, who was trying to dispense as many glasses as she could to a crowd of waiting guests.

The muttering organizer scurried towards her, showing how she should present the drinks.

'The drinks are on the table,' she grumbled out of the corner of her mouth. 'I don't see why they can't just reach down and pick them up themselves . . .'

'Because *you're* being paid to reach down and pick the drinks up for them,' the man snapped, and then smiled sweetly as a doddery Russian millionaire with glasses almost bigger than his face staggered away with the glass he'd been holding.

'We need to get out of here and find the others,' Harlan whispered to Jes. 'If they're going to crash the stage and announce it like we planned, we'll need all of us there or –'

'We'll be stopped before we've even started,' Jes finished, looking at the security personnel.

As Harlan looked away, he caught sight of Pyra and Luthan on the far side of the room. 'Jes,' he said out of the corner of his mouth. 'Look.'

Jes glanced up and it took her a moment or two to recognize Pyra in the black dress.

Talking quietly between themselves, Luthan and Pyra approached the table. 'Madam ... sir,' Harlan said politely, 'can I get you a glass of champagne?'

'I'd rather have a beer,' Pyra grumbled. 'I can't stand this stuff.'

Harlan surreptitiously raised his mask, enough for Pyra to realize who she was talking to.

'*You!* We told you to stay at the tower block,' she snapped. 'You kids don't listen to anything.'

'Maybe if you started including us we *would*,' Harlan whispered. 'And, besides, we've got a better opportunity than you.'

'A better opportunity to do *what* exactly?'

'To help you.' He narrowed his eyes at Stephen, some way across the room. 'You still want to take down the Pledge, don't you? Well, so do we, and we have a plan.'

Luthan shook his head. 'You both need to get out of here, before you mess up everything.' He gave Harlan and Jes a solemn look, returned his glass to the table and left with Pyra.

'Maybe we should just tell security,' Pyra said. 'They'd kick them out before they get in any trouble.'

'Or we let them stay,' Luthan pondered, gazing at the queue forming around the flustered pair. 'I don't know what this plan of theirs could be – I'm not sure I want to know – but a distraction might be exactly what we need to help us get our target.'

Pyra narrowed her eyes at him. 'You're gonna let them screw up so they get caught. Seems kinda heartless if I'm being honest, Luthan.'

'Then let's just hope we don't need to go there,' Luthan answered coolly.

Guess this is why Henry chose you to be leader in his absence, Pyra thought, but said nothing.

'Ladies and gentlemen,' the host announced amid the chatter a few minutes later. 'The show will be starting soon. If you would now like to take your seats on the balcony . . .'

The guests shuffled into a queue and filed out of the room.

'I'm not going anywhere except to find the others,' Jes muttered to Harlan. 'As soon as the show starts we'll head down to the stage and we'll find them.'

59

Luthan watched as Stephen stroked the fox mask on his lap.

'At least we know what Stephen will be wearing later,' he murmured. 'If Felix doesn't arrive, we should switch our focus to Nover.'

Pyra nodded. 'Agreed.' They watched as the actors quickly took their places on the stage. 'I'm bored already,' she said. 'Bring on the masquerade so we can get our hostage and get out of here.'

'Just be quiet and enjoy it,' Luthan whispered, not taking his eyes off Stephen. 'Besides, a bit of culture won't hurt.'

'Call this culture?' she snorted. 'A few of those actors look like they've been dragged in off the street. Hang on a minute ...'

'What's wrong?'

Pyra sat up straight, picking up the binoculars from the seat in front. 'Is that ... Ryan and Elsa ... and Julian? What are they playing at?'

Luthan reached for his own binoculars. He confirmed

her suspicion with a sigh and put the binoculars to one side.

'Ryan can't act to save his life,' she whispered. 'Look at him, he doesn't have a clue what's going on. Elsa's just bobbing her head around like there's something wrong with her. She thinks she's in a school play . . .'

Luthan muttered despairingly, 'Never mind their acting skills. They're drawing too much attention to themselves.'

He climbed out of his seat, encountering a chorus of tuts, while Pyra followed him back into the empty VIP area. Harlan and Jes were sat on the table talking quietly.

'Back already?' asked Jes. Her black mask was perched atop her brow.

'Have you seen who's on stage?' Pyra asked, nodding to the window.

Jes and Harlan got up and peered through the glass window. Ryan, it seemed, had given up entirely, sitting humorously on a barrel with his head in his hands while the director gestured frantically at him from the wings. Elsa was scurrying back and forth.

'I know we said we were going to crash the performance, but I didn't think it'd be like this,' Jes said.

'Hold on,' Pyra said. 'What do you mean, you were going to *crash* the performance?'

'We were going to tell the crowd what happened to us,' Harlan explained. 'We were going to expose the Pledge!'

'So *this* was your plan.' Pyra sighed, shaking her head.

Harlan turned to find the event organizer watching him.

The man looked at the ibis held menacingly in Jes's hands and then at each of the group in turn. 'What is going on here?'

'A simple misunderstanding,' Luthan cut in. 'I assure you we're –'

'You can explain it to security as they escort you out.' The man hurried nervously to the telephone.

Pyra snatched the ibis from Jes, pointed it and fired before he was able to remove it from the hook.

'In here,' Harlan said, pulling aside the velvet drape that concealed the cupboard.

Harlan and Luthan quickly dumped the man inside with the other two unconscious bodies.

'You two starting a collection or something?' Pyra quipped.

'We'd better head back,' Luthan said, taking the ibis and hiding it inside his tuxedo. 'We need to keep an eye on the Pledge. Meet us in the ballroom afterwards. Felix isn't here, so our target will have to be Stephen.'

60

Alyn climbed out of the car and opened the door for Felix. They walked up the marble steps, Felix adjusting his white scarf, and entered through the main doors. A startled attendant immediately rushed over to greet them.

'Mr Felix, I'm sorry but you've missed most of the performance. If I'd have known you were going to be late, I'd have –'

'Nonsense. I've never liked this sort of thing. My assistant and I are here for the party.'

'Then let me take you to the VIP lounge. I can get you a drink . . .'

'No, thank you. I've arranged to meet some colleagues in the function room,' Felix said, with a knowing smile to Alyn, and checked his sparkling watch.

'Good luck,' Alyn said. If Stephen was as bad as Felix said, he would need it.

'Thank you, Alyn,' Felix said, heading for the stairs. 'Hopefully this shouldn't take too long.'

Alyn took a seat on a bench in the foyer and folded

his arms. There was no sign of Emmanuel anywhere. Alyn couldn't help feeling that, for now, that was probably a good thing.

Inside the auditorium a bored Stephen looked down at his watch. He cleared his throat and politely made his way out of the aisle. Blythe waited for a moment then left as well, followed by Antonia a short while later.

Moments later, Stephen, Antonia and Blythe entered the function room on the second floor. They moved to the table in the centre. Felix waited until Blythe and Antonia were seated.

'*Semper ad meliora*,' Felix declared.

'*Semper ad meliora*,' the others repeated, apart from Stephen.

'I declare this meeting of the Pledge open.'

'Yes, yes, get on with it,' Stephen said, yawning. 'I've got a spectacularly stupid show to finish watching. Although it was worth it just for the moronic extras.'

'I think they were drunk,' Blythe chortled.

'You think that about everyone, you daft old fart,' Stephen sneered. 'Not everyone's like you.'

'Come now,' Felix said. 'We're not here to insult each other.'

'Then maybe you should tell us *why* we're here,' said Stephen. 'You called this emergency meeting after all.'

'Yes,' Felix said. He noticed his hand was trembling. He looked at Stephen. 'This involves you.'

'Oh, doesn't it always . . .'

'I'll cut to the chase,' Felix uttered.

Felix looked to Antonia and Blythe for support, both of whom gave him an indistinct nod to continue.

'I have the great honour, Stephen, of telling you that working with you to get the project under way for the past couple of years has been deeply unpleasant. You're a thoroughly nasty, selfish, cruel, spoilt little monster and –' he stopped to catch a breath – 'the three of us have come to an agreement. Can I ask you both to declare your position?'

'You have my backing, James,' Antonia said, and cast Stephen a disapproving look.

'And you have this "daft old fart's" vote too,' Blythe added. He leant towards Stephen and patted him consolingly on the shoulder. 'Terribly sorry, lad.'

'That confirms it,' Felix concluded. 'You're no longer a member of the Pledge, Stephen. Any privileges regarding the project are gone. You have forty-eight hours to return your key. You are *finished*.' Felix spat these words with such zeal that a fine spray of spit exploded from his lips and speckled the table.

Stephen watched him, unblinking, unmoving.

'*Semper ad meliora*,' Felix recited. 'I declare this meeting *closed*.'

Felix walked to the door, but Stephen spoke. 'There's no rule about voting out another member, Felix.'

'But you're forgetting the most important rule!' said Felix. 'That whoever is the wealthiest leads ... and whoever leads gets to define the rules!'

Stephen furrowed his brow and brought a finger to his lips. 'But that's where this little plan of yours falls apart,' he said. 'Because you aren't the wealthiest.'

Felix turned to Antonia and Blythe and laughed heartily.

'Just before six o'clock this evening, *I* overtook you,' Stephen said.

'Nonsense,' Felix said with a laugh.

'Why don't you call someone? I'm sure they could verify it.'

Felix removed his phone from his pocket and noticed several missed calls from his assistant. He dialled the number back. 'What's going on?' he said into the phone.

'I'm sorry, James,' came the response, loud enough for the others to hear. 'There's been a bit of a problem. A butterfly effect . . . We're trying our best to resolve it . . .'

'You mean the businesses?'

'Yes, James. No one could have ever foreseen this would happen.'

Felix's voice grew quiet. 'Why . . . why has no one told me?'

'We've been trying to get hold of you but we haven't been able to get through . . . We've sent emails, left messages, the lot . . . James? James, are you still there?'

Felix ended the call and lowered the phone . He stared at it for a few seconds.

'Now,' Stephen said, clasping his hands behind his head. 'That puts me in a rather admirable position, doesn't it?'

'Blythe, Antonia,' Felix urged. 'We can still fight him.'

'Don't you understand, old man?' said Stephen. 'Susannah has been working for me this whole time at the prison!' He looked at Antonia and Blythe. 'If I can ruin Felix's fortune, I can do the same to the both of you. So choose your side wisely.'

'He's lying,' Felix said. 'Don't do it. Don't listen to him.'

'Antonia?' Stephen asked, delighted at Felix's distress. 'Blythe?'

Blythe considered this and looked at Felix sympathetically. 'Dreadfully sorry, old boy ... but I think you know what we have to do.'

'For the greater good,' Antonia added. 'That's what this was always supposed to be about, wasn't it?'

'Yes, but –'

'That's exactly what this is about,' Stephen clarified. 'The greater good. Not the crumbling ego of some pathetic, deluded old man. The Pledge lives on!'

Felix seemed to have aged another decade in mere minutes. He gave a half-nod, glared at the giggling Stephen, and walked slowly and quietly out of the room.

Alyn was still waiting in the hall when the doors to the auditorium opened and a flood of guests streamed out. Alyn got to his feet and slipped through the crowd, trying to keep sight of a stunned and shattered-looking Felix who had just emerged from the function room.

'Mr Felix!' Alyn called up, but was ignored. *What happened up there?*

'James!' exclaimed a man, putting his arm round Felix's shoulder. 'I just heard what happened, I –'

Felix shrugged him off and descended the staircase.

'Something must've spooked the shareholders,' another guest whispered behind his hand.

'What did you say?' Alyn said, turning towards the man who had spoken.

'JF Industries took a massive hit,' the guest said to Alyn. 'His business is collapsing.'

Alyn weaved through the crowd to the main doors, just as Felix was leaving.

'Mr Felix!' Alyn called again.

Felix turned his head slowly. 'I'm sorry, Alyn. I'm sorry. I need some time alone.'

61

'Thank God that humiliation is over,' said Julian.

'I hope you're proud,' said the furious red-faced director, pushing towards them. 'You've reduced me, the other performers and this opera house to a laughing stock.'

'Now if you're quite finished . . .' Julian said coolly and brushed past him, gesturing for the other two to follow.

'I wasn't *that* bad, was I, sir?' said a concerned Elsa.

The director stooped, bringing himself level with her eyes. 'You,' he said quietly, 'were the worst little girl I have seen in my life. And if you ever manage to sing a single note in tune, it will be nothing short of a miracle.'

'Oi, leave her alone,' said Ryan. 'Come on, Elsa.' He pulled her towards him and rubbed her hair protectively.

Elsa shrugged. 'Never liked singing anyway.'

Elsa, Julian and Ryan left the stage and found their clothes in a pile at the side.

'So what do we do now? We've missed our opportunity,' said Elsa.

'There'll be another one,' Julian said. He peered up the staircase at the ornate ballroom doors, where two attendants were hovering with trays of drinks.

'They're all in there,' said Julian. 'We should hold on until those waiters have passed.'

'I'm sick of waiting,' Ryan grumbled. 'I'm going in to find them . . .'

Inside the ballroom a string quartet exploded into a frantic overture. With her eyes on Stephen, Pyra slipped through the guests to the corner of the room.

Stephen must leave the room alone, she said under her breath, clarifying her intent while rolling the domino between her fingers. She closed her eyes and felt a crackling, fizzing sensation in the back of her mind.

At that moment a woman standing beside Stephen felt a twinge in her calf muscle, the hint of a cramp, and stepped back, nudging an older lady who was spraying perfume on her wrists. Diverted from its course, a tiny, almost insignificant cloud of perfume floated into the nostril of a tall man who was adjusting his eye mask. After a couple of moments, the man drew his head back and sneezed. Stephen, who was dancing with an elderly female opera singer, flinched to avoid the sneeze and knocked into a waiter.

The waiter's wine glass jumped in his hands, releasing a crimson splash on to Stephen's immaculate white shirt.

'Oh, Mr Nover,' he said, 'I'm so sorry, I –'

'An accident,' Stephen said, trying not to lose his

266

temper from behind his snarling fox mask. He looked at his partner and presented a fake smile. 'Excuse me while I clean this up.'

With that, he moved gently through the crowds to the doors.

From the staircase outside the ballroom Luthan watched as Stephen went into the toilets. He made sure no one was watching and removed the ibis from inside his tuxedo.

Luthan waited for a few more moments, then carefully pushed the door open and peered inside, where Stephen was adjusting the fox mask in the bathroom mirror.

'Got you,' Luthan snarled. 'And don't even try to move.'

Stephen turned slowly. The fox mask was sinister, grinning.

'The Pledge is finished, Stephen,' he said. 'It all ends here.'

Stephen raised his palms in mock defeat. 'You're making a –'

Luthan fired and Stephen's body slammed back against the sink and crumpled. He sped over and hoisted the unconscious young man over his shoulder.

'Luthan!' Pyra called into the toilets. 'Is it done?'

'It's done. Am I OK to bring him out?'

Pyra watched as two suited men marched past, following the corridor around. '*Now*,' she hissed.

Luthan cautiously backed out through the door with

a masked Stephen slumped limply over his shoulder. 'Here,' he said, and threw the ibis at her.

Pyra caught it with both hands. She ran to the ballroom doors and picked up one of the brass rope holders. She wedged it across the handles, sealing in the guests and members of staff.

She pulled off her heels and jogged down the carpeted stairs. Standing at the bottom with his back to her was a security guard. She aimed the ibis at the back of his head and fired.

'You're clear,' she said, beckoning to Luthan. 'Come on.'

She hopped over the unconscious man, only to be met with another security guard, who had just appeared from round the corner.

'Stop!' he called out, looking at the weapon in her hands as he reached for the radio on his belt. Pyra squeezed the trigger again and the man was thrown back into the wall.

She pulled open the double doors at the front of the opera house and squinted through the hazy rain for their getaway car. Pyra jumped up, waving. Anton caught sight of her and turned on the engine.

Luthan paused midway down the marble steps to hitch the slipping Stephen further up on to his shoulder and made his way to the car. The wind was fierce, lashing and whistling in his ears. Steam flowed from Luthan's mouth with the exertion.

Pyra, shoeless, was hobbling across the icy, rain-slick

stone pavement. She soon reached the car and opened the back door.

Luthan dumped Stephen inside and gestured for her to hand him the ibis. 'I'll go with Anton,' he panted, checking over his shoulders. 'Someone needs to make sure this one doesn't wake up.'

'I'll run back and get the kids,' Pyra replied. 'They're still inside.' She turned and sped back up the freezing steps to the entrance.

'This is very odd, I can't seem to open the doors,' said one of the masked guests as they rattled the brass handles of the ballroom doors. 'We're locked in!'

Jes watched the commotion. 'I guess that means the Guild have got Stephen,' she said to Elsa. She tore off her mask. 'Now it's our turn. Help me get the others. It's time we told everyone *the truth*.'

Elsa spun around, looking for everyone. She spotted Ryan standing by the wall. 'Ryan!' she cried, waving to him. Harlan noticed and threw his mask to the floor and joined the group. The last to see was Julian, who removed his ibis from inside his trouser leg and marched towards them.

A small crowd of guests were beginning to gather at the locked doors. The five teenagers grabbed one of the drinks tables and tipped it over. The champagne glasses and bottles rolled back and clattered against the floor with a crash. The whole room turned to see where the commotion was coming from.

Jes hopped on to the emptied table, followed by Harlan and Elsa. Ryan took his ibis back from Jes and stood beside Julian, with the weapons in their hands.

'We have an announcement!' Jes called, trying to make herself heard amid the confusion. 'Listen to us!'

A small number of people stopped and watched, while others at the front of the crowd continued to struggle to free themselves with increasing frustration. Harlan spotted a security guard speaking into his mouthpiece.

'Please stop!' Jes yelled louder until her throat ached. 'We have something important to say ... We need you to listen!'

'We were taken from our homes! We were kidnapped!' Elsa shouted. A few more of the pack stopped what they were doing.

'It was the Pledge! The richest people in the country. They did it! All of you have to help us!'

'I remember seeing you on stage during the performance,' said a man at the front of the group, pointing to Elsa. He moved his hand towards Ryan. 'And you! Is this some sort of joke?'

'We're telling the truth, I swear,' said Ryan. 'You've got no idea what we've been through!'

The crowd laughed politely and began talking among themselves until the room was once again filled with noise.

'This is very funny!' Elsa heard a woman guffaw. 'It must be part of the show ...'

'Ridiculous, if you ask me,' said another, pushing his way back to the ballroom doors to investigate the blockage.

'This is no good; they don't believe us!' Elsa said, frantically tugging Jes's arm.

Julian raised his ibis and fired at the chandelier. The blast *whomped* through the air and the chandelier creaked, swaying from side to side. The guests gasped and the whole room fell into silence.

'We came here to expose some very powerful people who are right here in this room,' Julian said, holding the ibis aloft. 'If you don't listen to us, our fate and the fate of all the others will be on *your* consciences!'

'Nonsense,' someone snorted. Jes, Elsa and Harlan watched the guests laughing to each other and begin to turn back to their conversations.

'It didn't work,' said Jes. 'Now we just look like fools! Is anyone ever going to believe us?' She put her arm round Elsa, who looked like she might be about to cry.

62

For several minutes Alyn had been searching unsuccessfully for James Felix. Shielding his eyes with his hand, he peered down the alleyway at the side of the opera house, half expecting to see the devastated billionaire slumped against the wall.

If something happens to him, he won't be able to keep his promise, Alyn thought, as the wind blew the lashing rain across him, flapping his tuxedo. His friends would still be in danger, the other children back at the prison wouldn't be released, and Stephen, the most dangerous one of them all, would be in control.

He brushed his hair out of his eyes and jogged back inside the opera house. A short way ahead of him he saw a girl in a black dress and no shoes sprinting up the stairs. She checked both ways, ran to the ballroom doors and removed the brass post that was holding them shut.

Pyra? he thought. He called out her name, but the girl was already engulfed by a mass of sequined dresses and tuxedos. Alyn fought through the crowd and entered the ballroom, where the majority of the guests were still standing. In the corner the musicians looked at one another, shrugged and began an enthusiastic rendition of Mozart's *Marriage of Figaro* overture.

'Pyra!' he yelled, pulling off his mask and throwing it to the floor. 'What's going on? What are you doing here?'

Pyra struggled to recognize him for a moment, then said, 'We're leaving, Alyn.' She waved for him to follow. 'Your friends are all here – Harlan, Ryan, Elsa, Jes –'

'J-Jes?' he stammered. 'Jes is here?' *She isn't dead . . . Felix lied to me!*

After their unsuccessful attempt to convince the guests of their imprisonment, the gang broke away to the back of the room to discuss what to do next. Jes scanned the crowd for the Pledge and her eyes fell on a familiar face pushing through the crowd.

'Alyn?' Jes said. 'He's here!' She began to run towards him, but Elsa got in her way.

'Elsa, what are you doing, get off me –'

'Stop, Jes,' Elsa said, grabbing her. 'He's on Felix's side!'

'Felix's side? No way. You're crazy, Elsa.' Jes tried to pull her off. 'Get away –'

'She's right,' Harlan said, intervening. 'You can't trust him, Jes. Don't do it.'

'I saw him with Felix and Blythe days ago!' Elsa insisted. 'I swear to you, Jes, I swear it . . . he's with *them*! You have to believe me. He's with the Pledge!'

Blythe had been watching the group's attempted announcement with amusement. He approached them with a sickening smile on his ruddy face, clapping slowly. 'Well, well, you naughty little rogues, fancy seeing you here,' he said, looking at each of them in turn. 'I don't think we've been formally introduced . . .'

Elsa jumped, and darted behind Ryan.

'Our men have been looking everywhere for you,' he said as he removed his phone from his pocket and began to dial a number. Ryan walked towards him and spat in his face.

Blythe wiped the tendril of spit away from his moustache with his sleeve. 'Charming,' he said.

'You're finished, Blythe,' Harlan said. 'You've got no idea what we can do.'

'Oh, it doesn't look like you can do much to me. You're nothing more than fodder. A tool. There are plenty more like you. Each of you is completely *expendable*.'

Ryan readied a second pool of saliva.

'Save your spit, boy,' Blythe chuckled, shaking his head, and marched away with his phone to his ear.

'The Guild has got Stephen!' Harlan shouted across to him. 'The project is over. You and the rest of the Pledge are finished.'

Blythe gave the group a lingering look of contempt and pushed through the crowd.

'If he's calling for help, we'd better find a way out of here,' said Jes, panicked.

'Get out of the way!' Alyn snapped at the guests, trying to fight his way through to Jes. He turned and then dizziness took him by surprise. He fell, landing on his knees. *What's happening to me?* He gripped his head, trying to focus his eyes.

He looked up and saw Pyra shouting at his friends. 'Come on, guys, we've got to get going, move it!'

Still unable to stand, Alyn clambered on his hands and knees towards the wall. He glanced up to see Pyra being shoved hard by someone, knocking her to the floor.

Behind her was a gang of men, muscular and clad in black. Each of them was wielding an ibis.

'Where are they?' yelled the man at the front of the pack.

'Over there,' Blythe snarled, pointing the teenagers out.

The men stormed inside the ballroom and closed the doors behind them. One stood guard, threatening the ibis at anyone who dared approach.

'We're trapped!' Elsa said, backing away.

'What in blazes is going on?' said an astonished man in the crowd. 'Is this a robbery?'

'It's all right,' said one of the men. 'You won't remember a thing . . .'

They can't get us if they can't see us, thought Julian, who had been watching everything from his position by the wall. He grabbed a fire extinguisher, removed the nozzle and sprayed, turning back and forth until the room and guests were half covered in a sea of foam. The panicked guests began rushing back and forth.

A gang member casually walked up to Julian, swatted the extinguisher from his hands and pointed his ibis at him. Julian took the shot in his chest and collapsed against the wall unconscious.

'No!' yelled Elsa.

Ryan charged at one of the men, tackling him to the ground and throwing punches wildly. 'I'll kill you!' he cried, furious and frantic. 'I swear I'll –'

An ibis blast silenced him. He crumpled and lay covered by foam.

Elsa threw her arms round Jes. 'I'm scared,' she whimpered. 'I don't want to go back to that place, I don't!'

'We're not going back there,' Jes said. 'We're gonna need fire. Harlan, do you think you can make it happen?'

'I'll try,' he said, and shut his eyes, ducking behind a table for cover.

Jes put on the best smile she could manage for a frightened Elsa and began hurling the bottles of spirits from the nearest table on to the floor. The bottles smashed on the ground and liquid bubbled and spread across the ballroom.

'Quickly, Harlan!' Jes said, only just avoiding an ibis blast.

Deep in concentration, Harlan felt the now-familiar light-headed sensation that meant the Ability was beginning to work. Just seconds later a stray ibis shot knocked a lit candle from a wall-mounted bracket. The candle held its flame and rolled towards the spilled champagne.

The floor erupted with a darting fire that followed the path of the fluid and rippled and writhed until great sections of the ballroom were burning.

The guests ran from the flames, shoving and screaming, and hammering at the doors in a great surge, knocking the man who was guarding them to the ground.

The leader of the gang raised his ibis at Jes. It was a direct hit, and Jes flew back and landed just centimetres from the path of fire.

Elsa scurried to the other side of the room, barely missing the ibis blasts. She watched as one of the thugs aimed his weapon at her, and shut her eyes. *If it's ever going to work, now would be a good time*, she thought, desperately.

'Blue elephant, blue elephant.' She whispered her locus over and over again, trying to help herself concentrate.

A single pearl from a broken necklace rolled in front of the approaching man's path. He placed his boot on the floor and skidded until his legs flew out from under him. Only as he hit the floor with a thump did Elsa open her eyes. *It had worked!*

Pyra, who was crawling on all fours between the foam and the flames, jumped on the back of one of the masked men, her forearms wrapped round his throat in a chokehold. She tightened her grip and eventually the man fell unconscious against a table, sending a tray of glasses to the floor with a tremendous clatter.

Pyra snatched his ibis from the floor and fired wildly, not bothering to aim at any of the shapes in the smoke.

Harlan raced over to Jes and pulled her clear of the fire. Then he ran towards Ryan and dragged him by his legs over to Jes. 'Someone make sure Julian's –' he cried, but before he could finish an ibis threw him off his feet. He rolled back over the table and fell silent.

There's no one left but me, Elsa panicked, realizing she was all alone in a room full of terrified guests and masked men, who were there with the sole intention of capturing her. She sprinted to the back of the room and hid behind a table.

Alyn, watching this, grabbed the wall to hold himself steady. He looked up at the men, who were standing in a circle in the centre of the floor, surrounded by snaking flame.

They're going to take them back to the prison, he thought, watching the chaos unfold around him. *I . . . I think I can do it. I can save them . . .*

Alyn shut his eyes and visualized the masked men fallen, lifeless and still. Then, in his mind's eye, he saw the image dissolving, turning into something. A shape. A butterfly, with burning wings.

'I can save them,' he repeated aloud.

He brought himself upright slowly. The imaginary butterfly he'd conjured as a locus ascended towards the top of the enormous brass chandelier, the centrepiece of the ballroom. There, among the wires and cords, the old, faulty electrics caught the flame from the butterfly's wing and exploded. The plaster began to crack and wither in the heat and the chandelier creaked and slipped a centimetre.

Alyn stood taller, raising his hands as though he was conducting an orchestra, feeling a subtle energy rising from his body. The chandelier broke from the ceiling, and plummeted on top of the gang, crushing three instantly. Two men were knocked unconscious, and the leader was sent crashing to the floor with a shattered shoulder and was trapped beneath the light.

Pyra looked up. 'Whoa,' she said, turning between the fallen chandelier and the boy. 'Alyn, what did you –'

'I don't know,' he murmured, looking at his hands. *I don't know.*

Seconds later the doors banged open and two members of the Guild entered, fighting through the flood of fleeing guests.

'Over there,' Pyra panted, pointing at the unconscious teenagers.

The pair ran inside, hopping over the flames, and picked up the limp bodies.

'Don't forget Julian!' Elsa cried, hopping from one foot to the next, not knowing what to do with herself.

Pyra knelt and hooked Ryan over her shoulders, battling her way slowly across the ballroom. 'Let's go,' she said, and grabbed Elsa's hand.

63

'Wonder if Pyra managed to get the others out of there?' Anton murmured, slowing at some traffic lights.

'I haven't heard from her,' said Luthan, gazing out of the window. 'She said she'd call ...' He removed his phone from his pocket and checked the screen.

'So what's the plan now?' asked Anton, gesturing with his eyes at the unconscious Stephen.

'I'll think of something.' Luthan reached over and touched the fox mask. Then something dawned on him. '*No*,' he spat.

'What's wrong?'

Luthan pulled apart the tuxedo. There was no sign of the spilled wine. He tore the fox mask aside. Beneath it was not Stephen, but a freckly, skinny boy with curly blond hair.

'He's tricked us,' Luthan growled.

64

Stephen, who had been hiding patiently in a toilet cubicle for the past half hour, was staring at the empty, devastated ballroom while sirens wailed in the distance. Blythe and Antonia stood beside him, wordless.

Broken glass and plaster littered the floor; tables were upturned and splintered. The lines of fire had died down to little more than a trickle of flame, but the room smelled of ash and dust. In the centre of the ballroom several of Stephen's mercenaries lay either dead, unconscious or injured beneath the enormous brass chandelier.

'Please!' cried the only conscious man pinned beneath the chandelier. 'I – I can't move . . . please help me . . .'

Stephen was about to speak but noticed Emmanuel standing by the doors. 'Thank you for the warning,' Stephen said with a smile. 'A shame it had to end like this!'

Emmanuel looked over his shoulder as a defeated, rain-soaked Felix staggered past him into the room.

'You all think you're so clever, don't you?' he snarled.

'Ah,' Stephen replied, clasping his hands behind his back. 'I was wondering when you might show up. You're looking a little doddery, old man. Would you like a seat?'

Felix ignored Stephen and looked at Blythe and Antonia. 'Cowards,' he said. 'The pair of you. Nothing but cowards.'

'Cowards who still have a place in the Pledge. Cowards who still have their fortunes!' Blythe stated.

Felix peered behind them at Emmanuel. 'And as for you ... you were supposed to be on *my* side. You're nothing but a liar ... a manipulator ... a snake.'

'Careful, Felix,' Emmanuel said.

Felix turned to Stephen. 'You're a fool if you think you can trust him,' he said, pointing at Emmanuel. 'He will play you off, one against the other ... He will destroy you all.'

'Have you finished insulting my adviser?' said Stephen wearily. 'Apologies, Felix, but I have things to do.'

Stephen turned and walked towards the doors, followed by Antonia and Blythe. Felix reached inside his pocket and removed a mobile phone. 'I had high hopes for the Pledge,' he said. 'But there was always something in the back of my mind nagging at me ... something telling me not to trust you ... any of you. That's why I set up a little ... insurance policy along the way.'

Stephen watched Felix with a raised, impatient eyebrow.

'Every meeting,' Felix said. 'Every conversation. Every

single shadow that each of us, including myself, has cast over the past couple of years, I recorded.' He held the phone up. 'Everything. There's enough material for you all to be locked up for the rest of your lives. Material that will destroy you.'

'And destroy you too, James,' Antonia concluded.

'And destroy me, Antonia. Yes. But it's a sacrifice I'm willing to make. After all, I'm already there, aren't I?'

Stephen smirked. 'He's bluffing. The old fool doesn't have a leg to stand on.'

Felix clicked a button on his phone and pressed the speakerphone.

'That data,' Felix said. 'Do you have it to hand right now?'

'Yes, sir,' said the voice on the other end of the phone. 'All hundred gigs. Do you want me to do as we said?'

Stephen, for the first time, showed surprise at hearing this.

Felix grinned. He began laughing, relishing the concern that was spread across the faces of the new Pledge.

'Sir,' said the man. 'All you have to do is say the word and it'll be public within a minute. Just as you requested . . .'

'Felix,' said Stephen, stepping towards him. 'Think about this very carefully . . .'

Felix backed away, laughing. He held the phone higher in the air.

'Felix!' yelled Blythe. 'If you say one word, I swear I'll throttle you with my own bloody hands . . .'

'Sir? What do you want me to do?'

'James,' Antonia pleaded. 'I have a family to think about . . .'

'James,' Stephen repeated more softly, advancing gently. 'Don't do it. *Semper ad meliora.* Towards better things . . .'

Felix, shoulders shaking with laughter, lowered his mouth to the phone.

Until that point, Emmanuel had been serenely watching the scene unfold. He closed his eyes, raised a hand in the air, gradually unfolding his fingertips towards Felix.

Felix opened his mouth to give his assistant the order, but spluttered. He clutched his chest and the phone fell from his hand, landing on a tangled tablecloth.

Emmanuel walked towards him. Felix dropped to his knees, wheezing and grabbing at his shirt. His face had turned pale and sweat was pouring from his forehead.

'I . . . I can't breathe,' Felix whispered. 'My chest . . . Please help me.'

Emmanuel clenched his fingers into a fist and Felix gave a sharp, sudden gasp and lay still. His blue eyes were wet and frightened and his mouth hung open.

Emmanuel reached down and picked up the phone. 'I've changed my mind,' he said. 'Destroy it. All of it.'

'*Yes . . . sir,*' said the voice on the other end after a pause. '*At once.*'

'So you have the Ability as well,' Stephen said as Emmanuel walked past.

'For someone who thinks they're so brilliant, I'm surprised you hadn't already guessed.' Emmanuel looked at the group of bewildered faces and quietly left.

65

Alyn had been hiding behind a fallen table. He waited for the Pledge to leave and hurried across the floor. Unmoving in the centre of the room was James Felix.

'Mr Felix!' Alyn shouted, rushing over to him. He ducked down, patting the side of his face and trying to stir him into consciousness. When he realized it wasn't working, Alyn interlocked his fingers on Felix's chest. He began pressing vigorously, willing him to splutter awake in a fit of coughs, like he had seen in countless films. He gave Felix one last futile push and closed his eyes, shaking his head.

Alyn brushed his hair out of his eyes and looked at the broken chandelier and the men beneath who were also motionless. They'd been crushed. *Did I really do that?* Alyn thought, and wondered if he should be feeling some kind of emotion, but there was nothing at all except a blanket of numbness. He quickly averted his eyes from the chandelier and back to Felix when he noticed something sticking out of Felix's pocket. Alyn reached inside and removed it.

A brass key. Alyn turned it back and forth. It was about twenty centimetres in length with a decorative handle. *I wonder what this is for?*

Alyn examined the handle, which looked like it was screwed on. He unscrewed it and peered inside the shaft of the key and found a piece of tightly rolled paper. He turned the key upside down, tapped it a few times and the scroll of paper fell to the floor. Alyn picked it up and unrolled it.

51.51

What does that mean? He turned the paper over a few times, hoping to find some further clue.

It was a few moments before Alyn became aware that a fire engine and ambulance had arrived outside the opera house. He shoved the key and the piece of paper into his pocket and hurried from the ballroom.

66

Morning light was falling through the windows of the tower block. 'I feel like I've got the worst hangover in the world,' said Ryan, rolling on to his side.

'You're too young to know what a hangover feels like,' Pyra said. '*Aren't you*, Ryan?'

'Yeah. Of course.' He sat up, rubbing his eyes. 'I remember the opera house ... I remember the ballroom ...'

'You don't remember your starring role on stage then?'

Ryan flopped back against the pillow. 'Crap. I forgot about that. So where are the others?' he asked, wanting to change the subject. 'Where's Jes? Is she OK?'

'She's fine. They're all fine. Elsa's the only one of you who remained standing.'

'Because she's so small, no one could hit her.'

'Excuses, excuses,' Pyra said. 'Come on. They're all waiting.'

Ryan stumbled out of bed and followed the corridor,

passing the locked room. He paused, thinking he could hear a weak groaning coming from inside.

'Hello?' Ryan said, and waited for a response. Eventually he shrugged it off and went into the dining area.

'Whoa, déjà vu,' he said, noticing them all sitting round the table with Luthan, Anton and Pyra. Several other members of the Guild were stood at the far end of the room, including the two men who had helped save them from the fire last night.

'What did you just say?' asked Luthan.

'Nothing,' Ryan grumbled. 'Just – nothing. Jeez.' *Can't say anything without you lot jumping down my throat.*

He sat on a chair, next to a sleepy-looking Jes. Elsa was bouncing up and down excitedly. 'Hey, Ryan, want to see –'

'A magic trick? Already told you I don't like magic tricks. You know that.'

'I was about to ask if you wanted to see the paper, weirdo.' She thrust a newspaper towards him. 'Look.'

'*Country's former richest man dies in ballroom blaze,*' he read. 'Felix is dead?'

'Yep. They're saying he had a heart attack after he set the ballroom on fire.'

'No security footage then?'

Anton shook his head. 'I'll bet the Pledge had a hand in that.'

'Which suits us perfectly,' Luthan added. 'Otherwise Pyra and myself might be facing a kidnapping charge.'

Ryan threw the newspaper back at Elsa. 'So you managed to get that Stephen guy then? Where is he?'

'We got the wrong man,' said Luthan. 'The little sneak sussed something was going on and gave his mask to someone else. The Pledge may be minus Felix, but Nover is still out there, and he's the dangerous one. The project is still running.'

'So what now?' Jes asked.

'You can stay here with us,' Luthan said, 'all of you. We train you – *properly* – so you can join us. And help us defeat them. If that's what you want.'

'I'm not interested in learning the Ability,' said Julian, who was sitting on a chair by himself. It was the first thing he had said all morning. 'I don't want it. I don't need it. You know what the real ability is? Intelligence. Versatility. *Planning.*'

Pyra studied him with some interest before saying, 'Why did you come back, Julian?'

'So I could help you defeat the Pledge,' he said, steepling his fingers. 'And I still might, unless of course they don't convince me otherwise.' He gave the faintest smile to show that he was joking and turned back to the window.

Luthan got up, walked over to Pyra and leant down to her ear. 'Can I speak to you about something? In private?'

She nodded, and followed him out of the room. When

they were out of earshot, Luthan said, 'You didn't tell me what happened to those mercenaries.'

'Yeah I did – a chandelier fell on them.'

'But something, or someone, *caused* it to fall. You know as well as I do something like that is beyond any of our powers. Who was responsible?'

'Alyn.'

Luthan scratched his chin. 'You think he's been manipulated? He could be a powerful asset.'

'He's not some tool that you can just use, Luthan. He's a person. A sixteen-year-old.'

'Of course,' Luthan said with a smile. 'But a weapon too. We need to find him as soon as possible. If we're going to succeed, we need him on our side.'

'And Henry?'

'Without Stephen as our bargaining chip, Henry will have to sit tight in Nowhere for now. He was aware of the risks when he chose to go there.'

'In other words, you don't have a plan.'

'Not yet,' Luthan replied. 'But I didn't spend twenty years in the military for nothing.'

'The kids did well last night, though,' said Pyra. 'Maybe we should cut them some slack.'

Luthan considered this. 'Perhaps,' he said, 'but for now, they have one more test ahead of them.'

67

Susannah waited for Stephen at the prison gates. He wore a designer hooded anorak and a scarf that covered the lower part of his face.

'My visitor,' Susannah said to the guard, who nodded and stepped aside. The pair went through the gates and trudged across the deserted exercise yard.

'Oh yes, the air feels *different* here,' Stephen said, extending his hand, as though checking for rain. 'Don't you feel that, Ms Dion?' He began gently moving his fingers, as if he was strumming an invisible harp.

They soon reached her office, which was piled high with cinema reels, cardboard boxes and a projector balanced precariously on a tower of hardback books.

Stephen sat and pulled his hood back. 'Felix may have taken a more relaxed view of the project but now *I'm* in charge of the Pledge and I run things differently. I understand that since the project started, you've been doing three, somewhat minor, manipulations per week . . .'

Susannah nodded. 'Not including the extra work I've been doing for you to bring down Felix's business.'

Ignoring this, Stephen plucked a notepad and a pen from inside his coat. 'Give me a standard week. As an example.'

'The planned terrorist threats. We showed the subjects a spliced image of a bomb malfunctioning and –'

'And it worked. The attack didn't go as planned.'

'Yes, sir.'

Stephen jotted something down, licked his finger and turned the page. 'And what else?'

'We've been gradually boosting the economy each week –'

'Yes,' he said with a sigh, scribbling something else. 'And what else?'

'Foreign relations,' she said. 'You know the deal with the –'

'What else?'

'The Mayor's speech at City Hall. The protestors were threatening to cause a scene. We were able to harness the Ability to quieten things down a bit.'

Stephen considered making a note, but instead snapped his pen closed and slotted his notebook back inside his coat.

'It's nothing short of a miracle that Felix got to where he did, and lasted as *long* as he did,' he said. 'Stopping parliamentary riots? If anything, I'm all for them! Should things take a turn for the worse, it'll just be one less interfering politician!' He got up from his chair. 'Running a country is like running a business. *I'm* now the most successful businessman in the country, so it's only fair that I run the country too.'

'I see,' Susannah said uncomfortably.

'And all this talk about "boosting the economy" – what are you really doing? Adding another zero on to some hideous little economist's spreadsheet? Nonsense! The problem with the country, as I see it, is that there are simply too many people fighting over too few resources. And what happens? People keep breeding, and breeding . . .'

Stephen sat on Susannah's desk and clasped his hands together. 'Not that you'd know anything about it, Ms Dion, but when a business suffers we usually start by making redundancies. By cutting staff. That is precisely what we need to do for the sake of the country. With fewer people we have more resources, more jobs. More potential for growth. There's always plenty of room in utopia!'

'You want me to harness the children's Ability to . . . *remove* some of the population?'

'Yes,' he said, giggling. 'That is exactly what I want you to do!'

'That would be mass murder!' Susannah said, aghast.

Ignoring her, Stephen said, 'There are, what, seventy million in the country? Let's start with around a third of that. Twenty million!' he squealed. 'It could be a virus, some weather-related thing, I don't care. I'm sure it wouldn't be hard to think of something . . .'

Susannah shook her head. 'No, Stephen. I can't do this.' She stood but Stephen grabbed her arm.

'Mummy and Daddy have always given me everything I want. I'm used to getting my own way, and no one interferes with that . . . not the Pledge, not Felix, and not you, Ms Dion!'

'No, Stephen,' she said. 'This is murder.'

'It's for the greater good! Don't you understand, woman?' He shook her. 'If you don't do this for me, I'll see to it that the first head to roll is yours!'

Susannah covered her eyes with her hand and started to sob.

Stephen let go of her, pointing at her and yelping with delight. 'I made you cry!' he shrieked, his eyes wide, childlike and excited. 'You'll do it, Ms Dion, or I'll find someone else who can!'

Giggling behind his hand like a naughty infant, Stephen left her office and ran outside through the snow.

He knelt by the yard door, gathered a ball of snow and threw it at one of the unsuspecting guards, laughing until he was gripping his sides and he could barely breathe.

Epilogue

Alyn wandered through the freezing streets, slipping in and out of the dashing pedestrians. In his mind's eye he watched the chandelier fall amid the smoke and fire; he could hear the creak of plaster loosening and then the screams from the masked men below.

He felt his breath escape him as though drowning and came to. Alone on a bustling street. The sky was overcast and threatened rain. He removed Felix's key from his pocket. *What next?* he thought.

'Out of the way,' someone growled and pushed past.

Alyn stepped inside a department-store doorway and put his hand to his head. He closed his eyes, but again the scene played.

He jumped as the chandelier fell, and looked up to find a hand on his shoulder.

'You,' Alyn hissed.

Emmanuel slipped his hands inside his overcoat pockets.

'Felix is dead,' Alyn said. 'They say it was a heart attack but I know it wasn't. I know he was killed.'

'Quite a claim, Alyn. I hope you have the evidence.'

'I'll find it,' Alyn said. He pulled back, staring at Emmanuel. 'What do you want? And who are you?'

'Who I am is irrelevant. I'm setting something in motion, Alyn. Something great ... and wonderful. Something that no one could have ever dreamed of.'

'The Pledge says the same sort of stuff,' Alyn sneered.

'The Pledge has no idea what I can do or what you can do. I want you to join me,' Emmanuel said. 'And you'll have no reason to be scared.'

'Join you?'

'The Pledge thinks that by harnessing the Ability through you, and the rest of the prisoners, they can save the country. But all they're really doing is putting a plaster over a wound that will never heal. Everything needs to be destroyed, Alyn. Incinerated. So that a new age can be rebuilt from the ashes.'

'And you plan on doing this *how* exactly?'

'I don't plan on doing anything. It has already begun. Join me, Alyn.'

He extended his hand towards the boy. Alyn looked down at his hand, then back up at Emmanuel, who was smiling.

Acknowledgements

Just weeks before *Nowhere* was released, a very anxious and excited me made the mistake of saying, 'Wow – this must be how a pregnant woman feels!' to a room full of women, many of whom had children. It did not go down well. Looking back, it was the wrong thing to say – not even because of a typical male trivializing of the pain of childbirth – but because the creation of a novel is not at all a singular effort. It is a collaboration.

And so for that I would like to sincerely thank everyone at Puffin Books who I previously mentioned for their *amazing* contributions, guidance and support. I really am tremendously lucky and grateful every single day to be a part of the family.

Also, a massive thanks again to my amazing agent Claire Wilson and everyone else at RCW and to Bella Pearson, for all of her editorial assistance with this book. (Oh, and to Sarah, who would probably kill me if I didn't mention her.)

**FIND OUT WHAT HAPPENS
NEXT IN THE SERIES FINALE**

SOME
WHERE

COMING 2015